AURIC

A CRASHLAND COLONY ROMANCE

LESLIE CHASE

AURIC

Editing by Sennah Tate

Copyright 2019 Leslie Chase
All rights reserved

This is a work of fiction intended for mature audiences. All names, characters, businesses, places, events and incidents are products of the author's imagination. Any resemblance to actual persons, living or dead, or actual events is purely coincidental.

❦ Created with Vellum

Dedicated to the Saucy Words writing group, without whom this book might not have been written and would certainly have taken twice as long! Thanks for the support, folks!

1

TAMARA

Above the deck of the *Wandering Star*, a sunrise blossomed. Beautiful, eternal, shining. A vast bright light dominating the sky, far larger and brighter than any sunrise seen on Earth. The first time I'd seen it, I'd thought it was beautiful.

Now it just meant I was late. I grumbled under my breath as I stepped out onto the deck, protected from the vacuum by the ship's forcefield, hurrying across the open space towards the tower of the bridge.

I'd spent too long trying to work on my actual job in the engine room and now I'd be in trouble when I didn't arrive for the pointless make-work on time.

Bright white light shone through the invisible dome of the forcefield that kept in the air aboard the *Wandering Star*. The old ship's solar collector wings were spread wide, charging the ship's batteries until we had enough to jump to the next star on our course. After each jump we needed weeks to recharge our ancient, rented hyperdrive. A newer, smaller model could charge in days or even hours, but there was no way that the Arcadia Colony Company could afford something like that.

Once we arrived at our destination, the deck would be full of life. I'd seen the plans, back on Earth before we set out — the *Wandering Star* would set down on Arcadia and form the center of the new colony. A market, a forum, a gathering place, somewhere for the colonists and their families to gather and talk. Somewhere they could enjoy themselves.

All of that was packed away for the trip. There were only five of us awake to crew the giant ship and the vast deck felt empty. *Was* empty, with the colonists in stasis in their colony pods, stored like so much cargo, waiting for Arrival Day. Then the pods would land all around our new home while the *Wandering Star* itself became the colony's hub.

The pods ranged from small, single-family ships to giant craft carrying thousands of colonists. Altogether the *Wandering Star* carried over a hundred thousand human souls, and the five crew were responsible for getting them to Arcadia safe and sound. No pressure there, then.

"Only another six months," I muttered to myself as I reached the door to the bridge. "Six months and we set down on a planet and I can put all this behind me. Maybe I'll even find a friend to talk to."

Beside me, Mr. Mews meowed a plaintive noise and I looked down at him, half-grumpy and half-amused. The holographic cat was the colony program's concession to the psychological pressures of deep space, and while I didn't want to admit it, it helped. As a computer interface, he was supremely annoying — but at least he gave me someone to talk to.

"You're better company than anyone else aboard," I told him, feeling silly about reassuring a computer program. "Don't take it personally, but I'm looking forward to having some other humans to talk to. This trip's taking far too long."

Mr. Mews purred an acknowledgment, a soothing noise that made me instantly feel a little better. Using ultrasound to manipulate my emotions made me uncomfortable, but there was no denying that it worked. And we all needed something to clear our minds and keep us from killing each other.

It was the same technology that the companion holograms would use to keep the dangerous animals of Arcadia at bay when we arrived. I wasn't sure I liked the fact that the Colony Company treated its own employees the same way it treated predators, but that was a complaint that could wait until we'd arrived.

The journey to Arcadia was a long and winding one, jumping from star to star and skirting the edge of taveshi space. The Tavesh Empire was an enigmatic power, dangerous and uncommunicative. No one wanted to risk angering them by cutting through their borders — which meant, the colony's planners assured us, that this was a safe path to travel. No space pirates would risk their wrath, and that meant we were less likely to meet any of them in this region.

Honestly, I'd have traded a risk of space pirates for shaving a few months off our travel time. We were slowly going crazy on our own here, but there was nothing we could do about it.

Straightening my uniform, I plastered a smile on my face and pushed open the door. Best foot forward.

"Morning, McKenzie," I said as brightly as I could. The navigator looked up at me from the sensor station, glowering. It was never a good morning for him, and the end of a night shift would be worse than most.

"Tamara. You're late." His eyes narrowed, tiny in his fat face, and he pushed himself up from his chair. It creaked under his weight, and his own virtual cat hissed at me before he dismissed it. Every member of the crew had a virtual pet, and they took on elements of our personalities.

"Come on, McKenzie, it's only five minutes," I protested. "What difference does it make? Don't make a big deal about it."

He kept up the glare and I tried to look contrite. After a long, long moment, he sighed.

"You owe me one, then," he said, stuffing the book he'd been reading into his pocket and stretching. He grinned at me, or maybe leered, and I winced as his gaze dropped from my face to my breasts.

Yeah, I know how you want me to pay you back. But he wouldn't say it out loud. Captain Donovan might not be good for much, but there was one thing I'd say for him: he took harassment complaints seriously. This was his last command, and he didn't want his record spoiled by something like that.

So I glared at McKenzie steadily until he looked away and pulled an unhappy face. "Fine. You take fifteen minutes of my next shift."

I winced but didn't protest. That would be annoying, but I could live with it. And I *was* late.

Satisfied, he stomped his feet back into his boots and pushed past me to start his walk back to the crew quarters. I slumped into the chair he'd vacated, still warm from his body heat, and glanced at the scanners.

This was the worst thing about the long journey. There was nothing to do unless something went wrong, and we were all keeping busy with make-work. McKenzie was the navigator, I was an engineer, and neither of us had any jobs that needed doing while the drive charged up. So we ended up taking shifts watching the scanners, which was at least marginally useful.

Someone had to watch them just in case, but our orbit around the bright star was clear. The odds of finding anything were tiny, hardly worth bothering with.

I started a full scan to be safe, though it seemed pointless. McKenzie had run one six hours ago, and nothing should have changed since then. Recharging the *Wandering Star's* hyperdrive for the next jump would take weeks, and we were contractually obligated to keep a constant eye out for trouble.

Why did I have to ship as crew? Why couldn't I sleep my way to Arcadia? But that was an option for people wealthy enough to buy a share in the ACC or lucky enough to win a place in the colony lottery. Or those who had a patron to pay for their shipping — some of the colonists were shipping out under contract. Me, I didn't have those connections. I could barely pay for my contribution to the colony at the far end. Paying for the flight there too? No way.

That was the problem. All of the crew were like me, only here to pay our way off Earth. All apart from the captain, an officer past his prime, ferrying colonists at the end of his career. No one on the crew wanted to be here, and we were all grumpy after months trapped together.

"At least I'm learning something this way. Anything in the logs I should know about?" I asked Mr. Mews. He purred something from my communicator wristband and I sighed. As much as I appreciated the cat's company, whatever genius had decided that our interface with the ship should be a cute animal needed his head examined. Hearing him purr made me feel better, but it wasn't a great way to talk to the ship's computer.

It worked, though. The virtual cat scrolled through McKenzie's log entries, showing nothing of interest. Exactly what I could expect from my shift.

"Right, Mr. Mews, time to brush up on my Galtrade," I said, pulling out my phrasebook. The alien trade language fascinated me, especially since the ship's technical manuals were written in it. If I was going to understand the alien machinery I babysat in the engine room, I needed to have some grasp of the language.

I worked my way through some exercises, Mr. Mews correcting my pronunciation. Hearing a cat speak in an alien language would never be normal, but it did help me learn. And so did the little nuzzles he gave me when I got something right. The forcefield projector built into my wrist computer was just strong enough that I could feel him, and it made me smile every time.

BING. The alert pulled me out of my studies with a start. It took a moment to realize what it meant.

Frowning, I looked at the display. Yes, the sensors had found something. Something small, fast, and most importantly, something headed in this direction.

No. Most importantly, it was *changing course*. My mouth went dry as I realized what that meant. There was no natural explanation, it had to be another ship. An alien ship.

Either that or the sensors were malfunctioning. They were as old as the rest of the ship, after all. "That'll be it, won't it, Mr. Mews? The sensor dish is playing up again. Right?"

Mr. Mews looked dubious, and I couldn't blame him. The sensors were old, but this would be a weird way for them to malfunction. And I'd checked the dish a couple of days earlier.

Trying to control my excitement, I thought of other explanations. Maybe McKenzie had set this up as a prank. That seemed a more likely explanation than that we'd randomly met an alien spaceship. In the depths of space that would be as unlikely as winning the lottery every week for a year. I *couldn't* be that lucky.

But the virtual cat meowed insistently. I couldn't just ignore this even if it was probably nothing.

"Okay, okay, I'll check it again." Ordering another sensor sweep, I focused the *Wandering Star's* sensors on the area of space the reading had come from.

Mr. Mews meowed again, and I glowered at him. "I am *not* waking the captain for this. Not till I've checked it."

Just the thought of the chewing out I'd get if I woke Captain Donovan for nothing made me wince. He wasn't a fan of being disturbed, even if the regulations said I should call him at the first sign of alien contact.

Of course, if it turned out to be real, he'd chew me out for *not* calling him right away. I was in trouble either way.

Bing. Crap. Time to find out.

The sensors told me three things. One: we'd spotted a small ship. Two: it wasn't a human ship. And three: it was headed straight for the *Wandering Star* and accelerating hard.

"That can't be a coincidence," I said, hitting the alarm button and hoping I wasn't the victim of a prank. "If this is McKenzie fucking around, I *will* kill him."

2

AURIC

Hours earlier, and light-years away

~

"You cannot be serious," I said, staring in horror at the plan the other Alpha-Captains of the Silver Band presented. "The war may not be going as we would wish, but this plan goes against the Code. What use is victory if we win without honor?"

My fighter floated alongside the Silver Band's fleet as we argued over its future. It was a depressing sight — not that long ago we'd been the terror of space, mighty and fearless. Now, our numbers shrinking, we were reduced to this. A ragged fleet huddling around a heartstar to recharge our drives and make our plans.

Seven captains in council, arguing about our future. And our soul.

I had the Council's attention, at least. My reputation and my name won me that much, and my words made several of them uncomfortable. But with the situation this desperate, I couldn't be sure that they would listen.

"Alpha-Captain Auric, I hear your words," Zaren said formally. "None of us like this plan, but the Halverans press us hard. If we cling to our Code and die, who will avenge our homeworld? The human colony ship has all that we need to make a planet our own.

"More than that, we need mates. You know as well as I that our warriors must find partners outside our species if the prytheen are to survive."

The rest of the Alpha-Captains nodded along with that, and even I couldn't argue. The Halveran sneak attack had destroyed our homeworld, wiping out our civilians. All that remained were warriors and while we were more than a match for the Halverans in equal numbers, we had no way to replenish our strength.

If there was a hope that we could find mates amongst the humans, that would be a powerful draw to our warriors. One that would tempt otherwise honorable warriors to dishonorable plans. And here was Zaren, just the man to push us into abandoning the Code our people had followed for centuries.

A hologram of his face floated above the controls of my fighter, cold-eyed and hungry. Beside him floated the other Alpha-Captains, joint leaders of the Silver Band. The seven of us were equals in theory, and our decision here would shape the Silver Band's conduct in the war between our people and the Halverans.

Some voices were more equal than others. Alpha-Captain Zaren's influence had grown, and his voice carried more weight than most. It wasn't completely unearned — his clan had fought well, winning victories we sorely needed. But they won them by abandoning honor and the heart of our people's being, and threatened to pull the rest of us down that path.

Every warrior of the Band fought in battle, but each clan had its own specialty. Miira's pilots were the best in space, Vindar's warriors were famous for their ground combat skills. Terasi commanded our scouts.

The last two clans were different: Layol provided logistic and moral support to the rest of us, keeping the Silver Band together. And then there was Coran, whose clan's technicians kept half the fleet flying. Both were still warriors, but not front-line troops like the rest of us.

Gathered together, the remnants of the Silver Band's fleet was ragged and battle-worn. The war was hard-fought, and year by grueling year our resources ran low. Without a home base, we were reduced to patching up what ships we had. It wasn't enough — over time parts wore out and failed, despite Coran's efforts. My own beloved fighter struggled and others had it worse. I could see the temptation in the eyes of my comrades, the desire for an easy win.

I shared it, but not at the cost of our honor. My father had raised me in the old ways of my people, ways that I was starting to suspect the rest of the Silver Band had forgotten. Or that they were willing to put aside when it was convenient, anyway.

"The humans are not our enemies. If we can find mates amongst their number, excellent. We should approach them as friends, as allies, and strengthen both our species," I insisted. "Let them colonize their new world and we can meet as equals, offer them defense in a dangerous galaxy."

Would they listen? The promise of a mate was a powerful incentive to follow Zaren's plan. Even I felt it — the desire to find my khara, the one female fate had chosen for me. Though I had no desire to find her by attacking and stealing from her people.

Looking at the faces of my peers, I tried to judge their loyalties. Coran and Miira were both Zaren's creatures now, more loyal to him than to the Code. They would back him for certain.

I needed the other three to vote with me. A lot to hope for, but from their faces they weren't comfortable with what Zaren proposed. There was still a chance.

Coran snorted dismissively. "There is no time for diplomacy. Think what we could do with the resources they hold in their soft hands. We prytheen are warriors, not merchants to grovel before them. Let us take what we need."

"They are new to space," I argued, "and they have taken no hostile acts towards our people. Humans don't even have their own starships, they lease their technology from the akedians. To attack them would be as dishonorable as attacking children."

I was laying it on thick, but I had to. And it wasn't far from the truth from what little I knew of humanity — they were an industrious race, and in a few generations they might be players on the galactic stage. For now they were still weak. An honorable warrior did not plunder a target simply because it was easy.

"We won't be attacking their worlds," Miira said, trying to put a reasonable spin on the plan. "As you say, the ship is akedian. They are our equals, aren't they? Taking an akedian ship doesn't go against the Code."

There was nothing directly untrue about what she said. That didn't make it right, either.

"An akedian ship crewed entirely by humans might as well be a human ship," I insisted. "And if it carries the riches you say it does, Zaren, its loss will cripple the colony world they are traveling to. Thousands will die, perhaps more."

"Better thousands of humans than thousands of prytheen," Coran said, baring his teeth. "Our first duty is to our people, Auric."

Before I could answer, Zaren raised a hand. "Peace. We all hear your words, Alpha-Captain Auric. The time has come to decide our course by vote — if we delay, we will lose our chance to strike."

I ground my teeth but nodded. Hopefully my words had swayed some of the council of captains.

Zaren voted for his proposal, followed by Coran and Miira. I cast the first vote against. Layol, Terasi, and Vindar looked pained as all attention turned to them.

Come on, I willed them. *Make the right choice. The one our ancestors would have made. Victory isn't worth dishonor.*

Terasi was the first to speak.

"Auric has a point," she said reluctantly. "The humans haven't attacked us, and they are too weak to be good foes. Leave them be."

She didn't look happy about her decision. Her scouts had borne the brunt of recent fighting, and she'd lost her mate to the Halverans. It wasn't easy to give up a simple way to rearm the Band. I nodded my respect to her for the hard choice she'd made.

Vindar and Layol looked at each other silently, neither wanting to speak first. I glared at the pair of them: if they abstained it would be three votes to two in favor of attacking the humans. I needed their support to block Zaren.

I saw the regret in Vindar's eyes when he turned back to me. Guilt mixed with a stony determination not to admit it. My jaw tightened — I could see what was coming and had no way to stop it.

"Zaren is right," Vindar said. "The humans don't matter. We need their resources more than they do."

And with that, we'd sentenced thousands of innocent colonists to death. My heart pounded and I closed my eyes, trying to master my emotions.

This is wrong. Killing the innocent and the helpless is no part of the warrior's way. I could almost hear my parents' voices as they taught me right from wrong. Did none of the others listen?

A warrior stands between the weak and those who would harm them. That was the first tenet of the Code.

"It is decided," Zaren said, no longer hiding the feral hunger in his voice. For Vindar this was a regrettable necessity: for Zaren, a chance to hunt prey that would not fight back. "I will lead the hunt against the human ship. For the next few days it will be at heartstar 571 — I shall lead the attack before they can recharge and leave."

"No." I spoke quietly, but with enough intensity that the others all fell silent. Opening my eyes, I saw the six holographic faces staring at me. "The Silver Band exists to protect the weak, not to prey on them."

"The Council of Alphas has spoken, Auric," Terasi said. She sounded unhappy about it, but she backed the majority. "Whatever we feel about the decision, it is made. The Code binds us to uphold it."

She was right. We'd all sworn to obey the decisions of the Council — it was one of the ways our ancestors had stopped the endless war between our clans long enough to get into space. But what did it mean when the Council voted to break the Code?

If whatever path I chose meant dishonor for me, I might as well take the route where I didn't kill innocents. The humans deserved no part of what Zaren had planned for them.

I powered up my ship, fingers moving in the familiar ritual I'd performed every time I'd entered battle. This would be the first time I'd armed my weapons against the Silver Band, though, and I was surprised that my hands didn't shake.

Do the right thing, not the easy thing, my mother had always told me. This might be the hardest thing I'd ever done, but I couldn't let my reluctance stop me.

"Alpha-Captains," I said. "I will not submit to this decision. Do not test me."

Zaren's face was as still as a stone carving, but Coran's smile gave him away. They'd hoped for this — hoped I would balk at their plan and fight them. Rebel, leading my forces against Zaren's and giving him the perfect excuse to purge my followers.

"Don't raise your hand against the Silver Band," Terasi pled. "We will have to kill you, and you know that you don't have the numbers to win."

That was true. Perhaps one in ten of the warriors gathered here had sworn to follow me, and not all of them would join me against the rest of the Silver Band. If I fought, it would be a pointless, one-sided battle.

There were other ways to defend the humans than fighting. Turning my fighter away from the fleet, I aimed at deep space and pushed down the throttle. Engines roared beneath me as I accelerated hard, opening the distance as fast as I could. Jumping this close to the other ships would risk dragging them with me — I needed space between us.

"I do not wish to fight you," I said into the comms as the Council dissolved into shouting. Behind me, their ships turned to pursue. "If I have to, I will, but that's not my desire. I will warn the humans and get them to safety."

Heartstar 571 was too far away to safely reach in a single jump, but safety was the last thing on my mind. The ship's computer protested as I laid in the course and overrode the limiters.

If I burned out my drive getting there, so be it. I would save the humans or die trying.

Energy bolts snapped past my ship as the drive wound up to launch me into hyperspace. Zaren wasn't letting me go this easily, and some of my followers were maneuvering to protect me from his. The Silver Band's fleet dissolved into chaos behind me. Good; with luck, that would delay pursuit and give me more time to speak with the humans.

An energy bolt snapped into my hull, tearing through the shield and burning out sensors. Not a fatal hit, but I couldn't afford any more. Time to go.

My hand hit the hyperdrive switch, and the universe dissolved around me.

～

WITH A SNAP, I reappeared in reality. A different starscape greeted me, a single bright sun close by, and I snarled in triumph. Damaged from the hit, it was a miracle that my fighter had managed to jump across the vast distance between the stars like this.

An even greater miracle had led me to arrive in easy reach of my target. The massive akedian ship orbited nearby, soaking up the heartstar's energy and charging its batteries. My sensors told me it was nearly ready to jump, and that gave me hope. If I could convince them to flee, the humans might yet escape the Silver Band.

I glanced at the damage report that flashed up on my screen and saw that my luck wasn't all good. The thrusters were damaged. So was the communications array. And the solar collectors were ruined: even this close to a heartstar, my batteries weren't recharging.

That meant my ship wouldn't jump again. So be it — I'd leave with the humans or not at all. *At least I've got time to act,* I thought. Zaren and his minions would follow, but they wouldn't risk their ships as I had. Their jumps would be more cautious, slower, safer.

Which gave me time, but not much. I set my sights on the humans' ship and accelerated as fast as I dared — the sooner I could reach them, the sooner I could save them.

The ship ahead of me was typical of those the akedians leased to newcomer races — blocky, bulky, and primitive. Old and worn out, on its last legs. Easy prey for attackers, and taking a chance just being in space. Its drive would take weeks to recharge, and I was fortunate it was nearly ready to jump.

"Thank you, blessed ones," I said, hitting the communicator and scanning for transmissions. Nothing broadcast on any frequency I could hear. Were they blind to my presence? Or just slow to react?

Doesn't matter. I need to talk to their leader, and if they aren't answering the communicators we'll speak in person. I ignored the warning lights and pushed the thrusters further, impatient to reach them. Acceleration was unsteady and I grimaced at the thought of trying to do any complicated flying with my fighter in this condition.

I'd covered half the distance to the human ship before a scanner sweep caught me. Pathetic — they were hardly keeping an eye out at all. The humans would be no challenge to Zaren and his warriors.

If I was going to save them, I had to get the human ship out of the system before the Silver Band arrived. Otherwise they were doomed, and my hopes with them.

I flicked on the transmitter and winced at the howl of static that filled the cockpit. Error messages filled my display, and I had to mute the channel.

Wonderful. The blast hit the communicator. I growled, my fingers tightening on the controls as I fought down my frustrated rage. It could have been much worse, I told myself. If the shot had hit the engines, the hyperdrive, or the life support system, I'd have no chance of finishing my self-imposed mission.

But every moment counted. Zaren's forces were on their way, bringing death and destruction with them. If the humans were still here when they arrived...

I tried not to think about that. Better to focus on stopping them. Zaren would take a route that let him recharge his fleet at another heartstar, and that gave me time.

While I couldn't transmit, at least the receiver was

working. A distressingly long time after they'd seen me, a message arrived, weak and crackling. The human spoke first in some language I didn't know, and then in stilted, barely understandable Galtrade.

"Captain Donovan of the *Wandering Star*," the human said, his accent atrocious. "You? Stop approach."

Urh. How do the humans not know how to speak? Again I wondered if I was doing the right thing. To rescue these people who didn't even know the common language of the stars, I'd given up everything.

Everything apart from my honor. That would have to do.

Bracing myself for the noise, I tried the transmitter again. No luck. I could hear but not speak. My jaw tightened again as the human repeated his greeting. It sounded as though he was reading from a script. Even if I could answer, I doubted it would do me any good: this Captain Donovan wouldn't understand anything I said.

The ship was close enough to see with my naked eyes now. A blocky, bulky thing, it was covered in landing pods, hundreds of them. Solar collectors spread wide like gigantic wings, catching as much starlight as possible. Deep inside, the jump drive was soaking up that energy, readying itself to throw the ship across lightyears to safety. I ground my teeth in frustration at the sight. If only I could tell them to go *now*.

Perhaps, if they saw me as a threat, they'd run? The problem with that was that if I opened fire, I risked damaging something important. I powered up my weapons anyway — the humans ought to detect that, and as far as I could see, their ship was unarmed. Captain Donovan might withdraw rather than face even one raider attacking.

No luck. The broadcast came again, but nothing changed. I had to speak to these humans, and with my transmitter broken that meant landing on their ship. With damaged thrusters that wouldn't be easy.

I tried to match orbits with the *Wandering Star,* only for the thrusters to rebel with a howl of warnings. The damage was as bad as I'd feared and slowing down wasn't going to be easy.

Cursing under my breath, I tried to wring as much performance out of the engines as possible. The *Wandering Star* was coming up too fast, and my pilot instincts screamed at me to swerve. I held my course.

If I went past, it would take too long to come back around. I'd have to risk a landing now, and trust fate.

The large, flat expanse of the *Wandering Star's* deck stretched ahead of me, starlight gleaming off it. I aimed for the center, decelerating as much as my damaged thrusters allowed, and braced for impact. The cockpit's forcefield held me tight in my seat as the deck raced up to meet me.

Landing gear crumpled as I slammed into the deck. With a horrible grinding noise, my fighter skidded, and for a moment I thought I'd crash through the raised bridge at the rear of the akedian ship.

Hauling at the controls I tried to decelerate. The

thrusters barely responded, the ship's deck tore under me, but I managed to slow the skid. I just hoped it would be enough.

The last thing I remembered was the bridge looming over me as the ship slammed into it. Then blackness.

3

TAMARA

This wasn't the first time I'd seen an alien ship. Of course not. They weren't exactly common on Earth but getting a job on a spaceship meant spending time in orbit, and that meant aliens.

Even the *Wandering Star* was an alien ship, though it was the kind of cheap worn-out junk that the akedians would sell to us. One day we'd learn to make our own ships, something better than this. Until then, we were stuck with the cast-offs aliens would sell us, at least for interstellar flights.

The ship that had plowed into the main deck was different. Small, sleek, *hungry* looking. Like an eagle compared to the clumsy albatross we were flying. It was the size of a small airplane, yet it had its own hyperdrive. The *Wandering Star's* drive was bigger than the whole ship, and probably less powerful too.

My hands itched to get a look at it, though I knew I wouldn't learn much. Our training with the hyperdrive came down to 'follow the instructions *exactly* and never use it when the warning lights are on' — no one expected a human to understand technology like this.

They were right, too. Alien technology fascinated me, and I'd studied it as much as I could, but most of it was beyond me. And compared to the ship in front of me, the *Wandering Star* was simple. I could work on a hovercar like dad had taught me, but this was far beyond anything I'd trained on.

It was magnificent. Swept wings like a hunting bird told me the ship was meant for atmosphere as well as space. The thrusters drew more power than our entire ship, and I could hardly imagine the speed this thing could get.

There were weapons, too. I couldn't tell what kind — nothing as primitive as a laser, that was for sure. And a forcefield generator that would protect the ship from anything we could throw at it.

Which didn't help you, did it? I ran my hands over the sleek black metal of its hull, wishing it could talk to me. *What the hell could tear through these shields so easily?*

Some weapon had punched a hole in the hull, tearing metal like paper. I peered around inside the gap, looking at the mangled tech inside. Most of the parts I couldn't even identify: what little training I had focused on how to use specific pieces of alien tech, not on general principles.

"Well?" Captain Donovan said behind me, impatient and nervous. "What are you waiting for, Tamara?"

He hadn't used my title since we'd left Earth's orbit.

That wasn't singling me out — none of the crew who'd joined up to pay our way to the colony got that courtesy from him. Only people who went to space for the love of it counted as crew to Captain Donovan.

"I'm not exactly trained for this, Captain," I said. It didn't work the other way, of course. He expected us to show him the respect due his rank no matter how he behaved. "You can't just point me at a ship and expect me to know how to handle it. I'm not a first contact expert."

The Captain made an unimpressed sound. His perfectly pressed uniform was stretched over his gut, and his neatly trimmed beard didn't hide the extra chins he'd grown on the trip. We all had our different ways of coping with the long months of flight, and his were cake and sleep. This was the first thing to draw him out of his cabin in weeks, and he looked like he wanted to scurry back inside as soon as possible.

"Just get the door open," he ordered. "Whoever's in here came crashing into my ship and I want to see who it is."

Yeah, right. If there was a living alien aboard, our brave captain would run and hide, I bet. But if the pilot was dead, he'd be keen to claim the salvage. That would be quite a feather in his cap; any one of a dozen corporations would pay a fortune for access to this technology.

It might even get him command of another space ship and a chance to keep flying. *That* was something our captain hungered for even more than the cakes he loved so much.

I walked around the ship, looking for a way in. There was a hatch, but no obvious way to open it and I could feel Donovan's impatience building. Pursing my lips, I pulled a pry bar from my belt and tried to slip the edge into a gap.

No luck. It wouldn't budge, not even a little. I turned my eye to the panels beside it — there had to be an emergency access point, didn't there?

"What's the holdup? You're our alien expert."

My back was to the captain so I could safely roll my eyes. "Captain, I'm not an expert. I'm just interested in their tech and their language. I'm doing everything I can, but I don't even know what species these aliens are."

He didn't sound convinced, not that I'd expected him to. But I didn't care — at least this was a change, something interesting, a chance to look at an alien ship.

My pry bar pulled open a panel, revealing a lever with an angry red warning label next to it. At least I thought it was a warning — whatever it was written in, it wasn't Galtrade. It didn't look like any language I'd ever seen.

There was only one way to find out what the lever did. My fingers tingled with excitement as I gripped it and pulled hard.

With a hiss of escaping gas, the hatch popped open. A strange scent escaped, like a cross between dry grass and smoke, and before anyone could say anything I pulled my way up into the ship.

If I waited, Donovan would send someone else. No way I would let that happen. No one aboard the *Wandering Star* was qualified for first contact with an alien species but I came closest. At least I was interested in aliens, unlike the rest of the crew.

The space inside was larger than I'd expected, dark and still and cluttered. The crash had thrown things everywhere and I desperately wanted a chance to examine them, but first things first. The pilot. Was he hurt? Was he even alive?

I pushed my way to the front of the cabin and into the cockpit. Of the three seats only one was occupied, and I gasped at the sight of the man slumped in it.

Back in Earth orbit I'd met some akedians, the tall and spindly aliens who'd sold us this old ship. And I'd seen some other aliens, stocky prells and birdlike tuvonians. But none that looked like this. Even unconscious the pilot looked magnificent, a tall and muscular figure with deep blue skin and dark hair, well over six foot tall and not an ounce of fat on him.

I could tell because, for reasons I couldn't fathom, he'd chosen not to wear a shirt. His torso was bare and I could hardly tear my eyes from him. There was no visible sign of injury, at least, and his chest rose and fell in steady, even breaths.

A live alien of a species I'd never seen. With a shaky smile, I turned to let the others know what I'd found.

"What happened here?" Captain Donovan asked from the deck outside. "Pirates? Was he fired on?"

He sounded a lot more confident now that he knew the occupant of the ship was unconscious and unable to hurt him. And that there was only one alien aboard. Clambering up through the hatch he looked around as though relishing the prize that had fallen into his lap.

I tried to keep my annoyance in check. Typical of him to look past the injured man and see only the valuable tech — I was curious too, but priorities!

"Captain, we've got no way of knowing," I told him. "Whatever hit the ship was powerful, but that doesn't tell us much."

"Can't you—"

"*No*, Captain." I sighed, exasperated. "I can't work this out just by looking at it. Maybe, if we haul the ship into the engineering bay, I'll be able to figure something out using the sensors… but I don't think so. This is a job for an expert."

He harrumphed noisily and I pressed on before he could chew me out for interrupting him. "This man needs to be in sickbay. That's first. And the best way to figure out what happened to him is to *ask him* when he wakes up."

The captain looked around the messy cabin of the small ship and frowned. Waved one hand in the air.

"Right. Okay. Get him out of here and down to sickbay then," he said. "When he wakes up, interrogate him. In the meantime, find out what you can from the ship."

"Me?" I squeaked the question, then got my voice under control. "Captain, I don't know how to interrogate—"

"You'll do fine," he said, clapping me on the shoulder. Perhaps it was meant to be comforting. If so, it didn't work. "You know the aliens' language better than anyone else aboard."

That much was true, at least of the crew. Presumably some of the colonists also spoke Galtrade, but we weren't supposed to wake any of them until we reached Arcadia. And this would give me a chance to practice with an actual, live alien.

A warm feeling spread through me at the thought of that, and I tried not to let it show. It was embarrassing, but I had to admit it to myself, I was looking forward to spending time with that hunk of a pilot.

Assuming he's not here to kill us all. I tried to remember that he'd turned up here in a combat ship, and a damaged one at that. For all I knew he was a pirate, and the damage came from his last victims defending themselves.

A *sexy* pirate, part of me insisted. I felt my cheeks heat and turned away to look at the ship. At least my interest there was safer. Sure, there wasn't much chance I'd learn anything new, but it would probably be the only opportunity I'd ever have to examine an alien spaceship on my own. I had to make the best of it.

∽

THE NEXT FEW hours were amongst the happiest of my life, and the most frustrating. The technology of this little ship was so far advanced over the *Wandering Star* that I barely knew where to start.

It didn't help that so much of it was damaged. Or that everything was labeled in a language I didn't understand. Mr. Mews couldn't help either: the language wasn't in any database he had access to.

What I could understand was weird. The ship looked like it needed a thorough overhaul, parts worn out but carefully tended. It oddly reminded me of some of the cars that came into dad's garage back on Earth — cars that the owner loved but couldn't afford to maintain.

Eventually, the holographic cat meowed at me in a reminder that I needed to eat. One of the more frustrating things about him — though, once I looked up from my work, I realized that I was starving. It had been a long time since breakfast.

"Fine, fine," I told the hologram. "You can shut up now, I'll get some lunch."

He purred at that and I glowered at him, pulling myself out of the little ship's engine space and dropping down to the deck. Maxwell, the purser, stood nearby carrying a rifle from the ship's armory. I shook my head — there wasn't any danger from the ship now, but *of course* he was on guard. His suspicious gaze never left the ship, as though it was a Trojan horse about to disgorge dozens of alien warriors into our midst.

AURIC

The mess hall was as empty as always. The huge space was built for hundreds, which made it uncomfortable for our crew of five. I grabbed a sandwich from the dispenser — it claimed to be chicken, though from the taste I'd have guessed rubber — and hurried out rather than sitting in the echoing emptiness. Mr. Mews purred approval as I ate.

Rather than head straight back to the ship, I made my way to the sickbay to check on our visitor. I could poke that ship for months without learning much, but with any luck he'd be able to tell me more.

Inside, Dr. Orson paced back and forth. She stopped when I entered, shooting me an angry glare. I held up my hands. It wasn't my fault she'd had this extra work dropped in her lap. And anyway, wasn't a chance to look at an alien a good thing?

The alien himself was in the isolation room, locked away behind armored walls. As safe and secure as a prisoner could be. Which meant I'd be locked in with him if I wanted to look him in the eye while I talked.

"How's the patient?" I asked. Dr. Orson pulled a frustrated face.

"Fuck if I know," she said. "I've got no clue what species he is, let alone what his life signs are supposed to look like. He's not an akedian, and he's not a bauran, and he's not a liil. That's all I can say for sure."

"Is he going to wake up?"

She threw her hands in the air. "Probably? His injuries don't look serious, and he's got no broken bones I can see. His heart rate's slow for a human, fast for a liil. Brain waves like nothing I've seen before. Maybe he's asleep, maybe he's in some kind of coma, maybe he's just resting his fucking eyes."

Her frustration was catching, and I tried not to let it get to me. The last thing I needed was a shouting match with the ship's doctor — she might not be easy to get on with but being on her bad side was a terrible idea.

"Can I go in and look at him, then?" I asked, taking a deep breath. "Or look at his equipment, at least?"

"Knock yourself out," Dr. Orson said, pushing her hands through her messy blonde hair. "The captain said to let you interrogate him. As long as you don't mess with him, I don't care. But if it's his gear you want, it's on the table there — I figured better to keep him separate from it, just in case."

"Smart," I admitted. There was no telling what he might do when he woke up.

The equipment didn't make me feel any better about dealing with him. Several knives, a blaster pistol that looked big and nasty enough to burn through a bulkhead. A set of what looked like grenades. It was a small arsenal, not the kind of thing a friend would bring to visit.

But he was definitely running from someone. Maybe that's why he's so heavily armed? I shrugged. There was no way of knowing why he had this gear, not till he woke up and told us. Or until whoever was chasing him caught up, which might be better or worse for us.

I picked up the blaster, turning it over in my hands carefully. Heavy, bulky, and dangerous. I wondered just how much destructive energy I was holding in my hands — if it used the same battery tech as his ship, this could be an incredible weapon.

There was no way to tell, not without taking it apart and I couldn't risk that. Firing it was out of the question, given how destructive it might be. A spaceship wasn't exactly a forgiving environment to punch holes in.

The best way to answer my questions was obvious. I had to ask him, and I was running out of excuses not to go inside.

"Okay, Doc, let's see him."

"Let me know when you need out. I'll be right here waiting."

Dr. Orson put her hand on the scanner beside the isolation room's door and with a beep it slid open. Feeling more than a little nervous, I stepped over the threshold.

I don't know what I expected, but the reality was less frightening. The alien lay back, sleeping quietly on a hospital bed, sensors attached to his bare chest. As I watched it rise and fall, I couldn't help staring again. Muscles like that belonged on a bodybuilder or a model or something — not on an alien fighter-pilot or pirate or whatever he was.

The lighting here was a lot better than in his ship, and I could see details I'd missed before. Subtle black marks on his upper arms looked like they could be tattoos, or perhaps he'd been born with them. His skin was an inviting dark shade of blue, and I struggled to resist the urge to touch it.

His hands looked strong, powerful but dexterous. Long fingers ended in razor sharp claws. I swallowed at the sight of them. Even without his weapons, this alien was armed.

Stepping closer, I looked down at his face. Hard, well-defined features, handsome and strong, somehow cat-like. I found myself wishing that I could see his eyes.

What do you think you're going to get out of this, Tamara? I shook my head. Learning about his tech, his origins, his story — all of that would have to wait until he woke up.

I'd be better off trying his ship again, even if that was mostly hopeless. But something kept me there, watching him breathe, his chest rising and falling rhythmically.

What would that skin feel like? I wondered. Like a human's? Or would an alien be different? Slowly I reached out towards his cheek.

His hand closed around my wrist and I gasped. I hadn't even seen him move. One second he was lying flat, unconscious — the next, he held me in a vise-like grip I had no hope of pulling away from.

I was so shocked I didn't even cry out. Just stared, wide-eyed, as his eyes flickered open. They were a strange golden color, the pupils vertical slits, nothing like a human's eyes. I couldn't look away.

"*Voshen das?*" His voice was deep, a vibration I felt as

much as heard. He had to repeat himself twice before my brain kicked into gear and I realized I knew what he was asking. He was speaking Galtrade, though his accent made it hard for me to follow.

"I—I'm Tamara Joyce," I stammered, trying to pull back. No chance. His grip was far too strong. "Ah, I'm the *Wandering Star's* engineer."

For what little that was worth. I answered him in Galtrade, doing my best to make my words clear and easy to understand. I had no idea if I was saying the words right.

But his golden eyes lit up and he nodded, making a strange gesture with his free hand. When he spoke again, he spoke slowly and clearly as though to a particularly stupid child. I blushed but didn't complain. At least it helped me follow his words.

"I am Auric, *Hresh*-Captain," he told me. That title meant nothing to me, but there was a sadness in his eyes and he paused for a moment before continuing. "You are in danger, Engineer Tamara. All humans here are. Leave now, go to another star. Danger is coming."

"We can't go," I said, fumbling my way through with my limited Galtrade vocabulary. Captain Donovan was right, I probably was the best linguist aboard. That didn't mean I was *good*. "The battery is only half…"

I trailed off, searching my memory for the word for 'charged,' but he seemed to understand. A low growl filled the room, a sound full of menace that made me feel weak at the knees.

"You hurry," he insisted. Something else followed,

words too quick for me. He saw my confusion, snarled, and tried again. "Leave. Get to a safe place."

I thought about the warning signs on the engines and shuddered. Engaging the hyperdrive without a full charge? That would mean disabling every single safety system, and I wasn't sure I knew how to do that.

Even if I could, I had no idea where we'd end up after hitting the button. The *Wandering Star* needed a fully charged drive to reach our next stop, but perhaps there was a closer star we could jump to instead?

Not my problem. Navigation's McKenzie's job, or the captain's. "I will tell Captain Donovan," I said to the alien warrior, tugging at his grip again. "You must let me go so I can do that."

He bristled at my commands, but I didn't know how to make it a request. Those piercing golden eyes looked deep into me and it felt like he was looking into my soul. His grip on my wrist didn't loosen and I swallowed, trying to pull free.

"Do not just tell him." The alien's eyes shone with a frightening intensity. "They are *keshar vro das...*"

He trailed off, seeing my confusion. Tried again, more unfamiliar words. I shook my head, swallowing. I'd learned as much Galtrade as I could, but I'd focused on simpler vocabulary. Trade and engineering jargon I had a fair grasp on, and I could order any number of drinks. But whatever he was warning me about, it was outside of my ability to understand.

Maybe that was a good thing.

4

AURIC

Frustrating as it was, at least this human was doing her best to understand. I kept telling myself that as I tried my best to explain the doom that was about to fall upon them.

"The Silver Band are killers," I tried, keeping it as simple as possible. No sign of comprehension. Gritting my teeth, I looked into the human's bright green eyes and tried to convey the importance of this. "They are *bad men.*"

That got through, though it didn't carry the intensity I wanted. Tamara nodded quickly. I struggled to keep my breathing even. This human was unlike anything I'd expected to find when I came here, and I couldn't tear my eyes from her. Soft, small, beautiful, her ill-fitting jumpsuit did nothing to hide her curves from me. Her hair was as dark as the blackness between the stars, her eyes green as the lost forests of the homeworld.

My soul had burned for her from the moment that my eyes opened. It was all I could do to focus on my mission rather than her. *Calm breaths warrior*, I told myself. *If I am to save her, I must make myself understood.*

"You will have to, um, undock my wrist," she said, pulling at my hand again. Under other circumstances I might have laughed at her choice of words. "I will speak to Captain Donovan."

Reluctantly, I nodded and let go. Releasing her hand was uncomfortable for reasons I couldn't quite follow and had no time to dig into. But while she spoke into the communicator on her wrist, I had nothing to do other than look at her.

This was a distraction I hadn't expected, but one I couldn't ignore. The mating urge of my people was upon me, and my body and soul ached for her. Was this what it meant to meet my khara?

I growled. By the Starless Void, this was a distraction I didn't need. Though it made me feel better about my choice to aid these people. Had fate sent me here to find her?

Fate's ways are mysterious. No point in worrying about them, just focus on what's in front of you. My father's remembered words were always good advice, and today they fit better than ever. I concentrated on the human before me, letting my gaze roam her body. Wishing I could see her curves without the unflattering uniform.

Her voice was soft, like a rider talking to a skittish mount, and I wondered what her commanding officer must be like that she took such a tone with him. Either a cruel and brutal man who needed careful handling, or a coward who did not take bad news well.

Neither were the kind of leader she deserved — and the impatience in her expression told me that she knew it. I wished I could understand her words.

The human finished her call and turned back to me. "The captain will be here soon," she said, trying and failing to hide her exasperation. "I will go and…"

Her words ran out and she gestured towards the door. My instinct was to grab her again, to keep her from leaving. I fought that urge down. We would have time later, if we lived. For now it was imperative that I spoke to her leader.

Tamara backed away slowly, her eyes fixed on me. I couldn't read her expression — was she watching a dangerous predator, or did she find it as hard to look away from me as I did from her? My heart raced as I watched her leave the small chamber.

Once the door slid shut behind her, I sat back to wait, letting myself slide back into a healing trance and assessing the damage. The crash had left me injured, but I would recover quickly. That much, at least, was good news.

The bad news was that I didn't know how long I'd been in this room. What might be a clock looked down at me from the wall, incomprehensible units of time ticking by. My communicator would tell me, but the humans had taken that along with the rest of my equipment. A sensible precaution, but a frustrating one. I didn't know how long I rested before the humans returned.

Eventually, a section of the wall cleared, letting me see into the next room. There was Engineer Tamara, but this time she wasn't alone. It took an effort to look at the other humans instead of staring at her. There was another human female, this one with golden hair and an annoyed expression. Both deferred to the third human.

Standing back from the window was a fat man wearing a fancy uniform that didn't quite fit. *So that's their commander,* I thought, trying not to judge him on his appearance. It was possible to be an able commander while not being fit for personal combat.

"Hello? I am Captain Donovan, the, uh, commander of this vessel."

I sighed. The diffident tone of the human's voice told me all I needed to know: this man would be a disaster in battle. Still, I tried to be positive. This was who we had, and that was that. With luck there would be no battle to fight.

"Captain. Greetings." I spoke slowly and clearly. Saw him struggle to follow and gritted my teeth. I would have to do my best and hope enough got through. Keeping my words slow and simple, hoping the humans would be able to follow, I tried to explain.

"You are in deadly danger. The Silver Band are coming, and they are mighty raiders. Pirates who will take everything that you have."

Blank looks from all the humans. Wonderful.

Galtrade wasn't the best language for this, and none of them even spoke that properly. I tried again, as simply as I could. "You are not safe here. You must leave *now*, there is no time to fully charge your engines."

Donovan looked blank, but Tamara translated. It seemed that of all the humans she had the best grasp of the language. Given how difficult it had been for us to talk, that gave me a sinking feeling.

Captain Donovan cut her off before she finished and I felt myself tensing, claws sliding from their sheathes at the disrespect he showed her.

Calm. You cannot do anything about it from here anyway. Besides, tearing the captain's throat out would do nothing to convince the humans to listen to me.

"We cannot," Donovan said, speaking loudly as though that would help me understand. "The engine must be…"

He looked at Tamara and exchanged a few quick words with her in their human language before turning back to me.

"It must be readied before use. Or it will *void the warranty.*"

That last he said in a rush, repeating a phrase he'd memorized without understanding the words. It was infuriating. He cared so much about the warranty that he'd risk his ship, his crew, rather than break it? What kind of a commander was this?

One who doesn't understand the dangers he faces, I thought. That was the kindest explanation, anyway. If he had any clue what he'd be up against, Donovan would risk the jump. Whatever deals he had with the akedians, they weren't worth sacrificing the ship for.

Tamara looked pained as she listened in, but she didn't interrupt. And the other female looked lost.

"You must listen," I said again. "I am Auric, warrior of the prytheen. Alpha-Captain. Killer. On my blood and my soul I swear this — flee this system, *now*, or be consumed."

No. I'd lost him, lost them all. Too complex or too frightening, I wasn't sure. How could I make them understand the peril they were in?

I stood up, lifting myself from the bed with an effort and facing the window. My injuries weren't quite healed, but they were close enough. Outside, the humans were talking amongst themselves, their language harsh to my ears, and they paid me no attention as I strode to the transparent wall. Not until I slammed a fist into it.

The captain and the blonde female jumped, startled. Tamara, though, stayed where she was, unfazed by my actions. Her eyes met mine and I could see her mind working, trying to understand. Did she feel the same pull to me that I felt to her? She had to, surely.

The fates wouldn't be so unkind as to send me a mate who didn't feel the same way.

Leave those thoughts for later, idiot, I told myself. What my mate thought about me wouldn't matter if we were still here when the Band arrived.

I slammed a fist into the window again, making sure I had the humans' attention. Miming an explosion,

I pointed to each of them. Gestured a knife across the throat. Death.

They had to understand the consequences of staying.

"Leave now, save yourselves," I said. Slow, clear, resisting the temptation to shout. "Otherwise—"

Another mimed blade across the throat. That would be the kindest fate in store for them if my ex-comrades caught up with the *Wandering Star*. Zaren would likely have uses for captives, and I didn't want to find out what he had in mind.

But death was a fate I could communicate in simple sign language, and that would have to do.

The three humans paled, exchanged glances. Tamara put her hand to the window across from me and started to speak.

"What do you—"

She cut off as the window went dark, turning back into just another wall panel. Someone had separated us.

I hammered my fist onto the wall, shouting, demanding that they listen to me. Pointless. The humans probably couldn't even understand my demands, and if they did, they ignored them.

Snarling, I prowled the small room. There was barely enough space to stretch out in here, but I had to keep moving. If I stopped, I might think about what was coming. What fate waited for the humans when the Silver Band arrived.

It had been bad enough when that fate had loomed

over humans I didn't know. Now that Tamara was threatened, my anger overwhelmed me. I would find a way to protect her, I promised myself. She would not suffer for her captain's foolishness.

Even if I had to abandon the rest of the humans to the fate they refused to flee.

5

TAMARA

Donovan stared at the blank section of wall, his jaw working, and I tried to decide whether it was fear or anger that was taking control of him.

In my case it was anger. Anger at him for cutting the conversation short. For disregarding the warning Auric had brought us.

"Captain, we need to know what's going on," I said, trying to be diplomatic. "What if he's telling the truth and we're in danger?"

Donovan snorted. "He's bullshitting us. Don't let him fool you, he just wants out of his cage."

Dr. Orson made a dubious noise but stayed out of the discussion. *Great, Doc. Way to back me up.*

"Why would he do that? What does he gain?"

"I don't know," Donovan answered. "Don't need to, though. Probably he's planning on robbing us, or maybe he'd try to steal the ship. That's why he wants us to jump somewhere else, see? If the *Wandering Star* moves somewhere off-course, he can plunder it at his leisure."

I glared at him, but he didn't seem to notice. Did he think one alien warrior was going to try to steal this whole colony ship on his own?

Admittedly, from what we'd seen of Auric's muscles, the careful cat-like grace of his movements, I wouldn't bet against him. Give him back his weapons and he might well be able to take on every human awake. There were only five of us, after all.

But then what? Trying to run the ship alone would be crazy, and anyway I felt a strange certainty that he wasn't lying to us.

Of course, we might be misunderstanding everything he said. Galtrade had a lot of words for piracy — and wasn't that a reassuring fact? — but it wasn't part of the language I'd focused on.

"Captain, let me try to get more information out of him," I offered. "Even if it's a trap, it can't hurt to know more."

"Your time is better spent working on his ship," he answered. "There's a lot to learn there. And the *Wandering Star's* deck needs to be patched where the alien crashed into it. He'll keep till we arrive at Arcadia."

"But—"

"No. That's final." Donovan turned on his heel, marching towards the sickbay door. "This Auric can spend the rest of the trip locked in the isolation bay, and the colony authorities can make sense of his story when we arrive. They'll have specialists who speak Galtrade properly."

He drummed his fingers on the wall, thinking. For a moment I hoped he'd reconsider, but when he turned towards me, his face was set.

"You're not to go near him, understand? As soon as the drive's charged we'll be on our way and put this behind us."

With that he swept out into the corridor and out of sight, leaving me to stare after him. Dr. Orson made a rude noise and sat down. "Typical. He doesn't want to hear it, so he won't. Our fearless captain won't let anything get in the way of reaching Arcadia on schedule."

"So you believe Auric?" I asked. It would be nice to have someone else who did. But the doctor shook her head.

"I didn't say that. We're not even sure what he's saying, and look at his armory." She gestured at the pile of weapons on the table. "Would it really surprise you to find out he's a pirate?"

Pursing my lips, I looked unhappily at the heap of knives and guns. Okay, that was a fair point — if he came in peace, why did he come so heavily armed?

"There's no way to find out without talking to him," I pointed out. "Let me back in and I'll see if I can get some answers."

"Nope, can't do it." Dr. Orson didn't look happy

about that. "You heard the captain. And I need a good report from him or I'm not getting off the ship at Arcadia."

Like everyone on the crew, the doctor depended on Donovan's good graces if she wanted to make a life for herself on the colony. A bad report and she'd lose her permit and have to ship back to Earth.

Which won't help if Auric's telling the truth and we're in danger right now, I thought, but her expression made it clear that she wouldn't listen. Nodding glumly, I left the sickbay to check on my work.

There wasn't much to it, to be honest. The repair drones didn't need my help fixing up the damaged decking, and beyond that there wasn't much to repair. There weren't many advantages to working aboard a ship that humans didn't understand, but at least it made repair work easy.

I had an itchy feeling in my fingers, though. A desire to understand what I was doing, to understand the tech we'd leased from the akedians. Mr. Mews could control the drones as well as I could, and that frustrated me.

One thing I'd been looking forward to on Arcadia — as soon as the ship was on the ground, I planned to pull bits apart and seeing how they worked. Not something to risk while we were in space, though.

Once I'd set the drones their tasks, I sat down and tried to think of anything useful to do. Anything that might get us out of here faster.

"How are the engines doing?" I asked the virtual cat, and he cleaned his whiskers as the display updated. About what I'd expected: three more days to charge the batteries before we left. I fiddled with the figures, making adjustments and guesses based on the figures in the database.

In two days' time we'd have the charge we needed for our next scheduled jump. Maybe a day and a half if we were lucky. Donovan *might* take the chance and jump early if we could follow the established route. If I didn't tell him how many of the safety locks I'd have to override to get it to work, anyway.

If we wanted to leave earlier, though, we'd have to pick a different destination. I tried to imagine his face if I suggested that and didn't like what I saw. Especially this close to the Tavesh Empire — they were *not* friendly to intruders.

"Okay, Mr. Mews, where is in range if we leave now?"

The interface meowed piteously, making me curse the designer again. Sure, it was cute, but I'd rather have a clear error message.

"What does that mean?" I sighed. "I'd have to ask McKenzie, is that it?"

The fake cat nodded, head butting me. Fantastic. That would go well.

Absently, I mimed scratching the hologram behind the ears. It purred and faded out as I made my way back to the bridge.

For once, the captain was in his seat. Usually he was content to command from his quarters but an unexpected alien guest was enough to get him out onto the ship he commanded.

He looked up at me, frowning. "You're meant to be repairing the deck, Tamara. What are you doing here?"

"My drones are working on it," I said. "Nothing I can do to speed them up, and they'll call me if anything needs my attention, so I figured I'd take the chance to go over some calculations here."

His frown deepened but he didn't argue. We all knew the ship was mostly automated: human crew were needed to command it but there wasn't much actual work to do.

"Fine," he allowed. "Get on with it."

"I need some navigation data," I told him, glancing at McKenzie. The navigator sat at his station, for once with his boots on, looking neater and tidier than I could remember seeing him since launch. Maybe having the captain on the bridge made him uncomfortable.

"What is it now?" he demanded, glaring at me. "I've locked our course in, we're just waiting on the engines to charge."

"Sure, but where could we go if we left right now? With the charge we have, I mean." I put on my best smile, trying to disarm the tension in the room as the captain frowned down at me.

"Listening to that alien's nonsense, Tamara? I expected better of you."

"I'd rather be prepared than not," I told him, shrugging. "Besides, it's not like we've got much better to do with our time."

"You know better than anyone we can't jump until the drive reaches full charge. The safety protocols won't let us."

Give me half an hour with a wrench and I'll see to those safety protocols, I thought but didn't say. The captain wasn't the kind of man who'd like me messing with the engine room, even to give him more control of his ship.

Instead I stood quietly, not giving him anything to argue with. He could have ordered me off the bridge, of course, but Donovan didn't like confrontations.

With a heavy sigh, he gave in. "Fine. Mr. McKenzie, satisfy her curiosity."

McKenzie shot me an aggrieved glare. Not only did he have to wear his boots, but he had to work as well? I tried not to let my amusement show. His glare hardened; obviously I hadn't been completely successful.

Turning back to his console and muttering under his breath, he set to work. It didn't take long before the main screen showed a display of stars highlighted in green.

"There. If we jump right now, those stars are in range," McKenzie said with poor grace. "None of them are on our course, and any of them would add at least a month of recharging to our travel time. Most of them are too dim to be useful, and the best one is in the Tavesh Empire."

I looked at the display. None of the stars shown had names, just numbers. That wasn't uncommon — humanity had only been exploring space for a few short decades, and we only had a few ships rated for travel to unknown stars. The akedians were reluctant to outfit us with high-end gear, and no one wanted to blunder into an occupied system in a worn-out ship like the *Wandering Star*.

Which was why we stuck to our fully-mapped course like glue, and why Captain Donovan was reluctant to even consider heading out into the unknown. It wasn't just cowardice — there could be anything out there.

Not every star would do, anyway. We needed a bright one to recharge the ship from, and there weren't that many choices. Any star would work with enough time, but some would take years.

"Happy now?" Captain Donovan asked, looking up at the map with distaste. "No known stars are in range. Even if I trusted that alien, I won't risk my ship on a blind jump."

I bit my lip and tried to come up with an argument he might listen to. Without evidence, it seemed impossible to convince him, and I wasn't even sure I should. Sure, I believed Auric, but I couldn't explain why.

For some reason I was certain he wouldn't lie to me.

Great. And who else did I believe like that? I told myself this was different from the guys back on Earth, but I'd thought the same thing every time I'd fallen for some asshole. Maybe this time it really was different, maybe not.

Before I figured out how to respond, a loud **BING** took it out of my hands. The *Wandering Star's* sensors had picked up something new and I had a sinking feeling I knew what it was.

Cursing, McKenzie cleared the starscape from the screen and pulled up the navigation display. A dozen new contacts showed, and more flickered into existence as we watched.

We'd missed our chance to leave unnoticed. The aliens were here in force.

∼

ALL I COULD DO WAS watch, frozen in place, as ship after ship exited hyperspace. They arrived scattered around the star system, some a day's flight away, others under an hour.

A pattern that would let them search the whole system quickly, I realized, feeling a shiver of nerves run through me. It felt as though we were being hunted. Perhaps we were.

"Get me a channel to those ships," Captain Donovan snapped. He sounded decisive, and it was a shame I could see his sweating face. Without that, I might have believed he felt in control of the situation.

Slipping into the communications chair, I tried to connect. It wasn't hard, they were broadcasting on an open channel, and with a few flicked switches I put them on the main screen.

Another alien looked down at us, blue skinned and scarred. Golden studs protruded from his head, and his smile seemed more like a predator baring its teeth than a display of friendship.

"I am *Hresh*-Captain Zaren of the prytheen," he said in Galtrade, speaking slow and clear. "We seek one of our own, Auric. He is a *vresin*."

The three of us exchanged glances. None of us knew that last word, and I didn't trust Zaren as far as I could throw him. Which from the look of the muscular alien wouldn't be far.

"I do not know that word," Captain Donovan replied carefully, slowly. I plugged Mr. Mews into the communication station, hoping that he could find it in the dictionary database.

"A breaker of laws?" Zaren tried, just as the dictionary returned 'fugitive.' If nothing else, this adventure was doing wonders for my Galtrade vocabulary. I set Mr. Mews to download the entire database in case it came in handy.

"I see," Donovan said, visibly relaxing. Switching to English, he turned to McKenzie and me.

"That explains things," he said, relief showing on his face. "No wonder Auric wanted us to jump blind — he wanted our help to get away from the posse chasing him."

"Or he's telling the truth and they're using this

excuse to get close to the *Wandering Star*," I protested. "We can't just trust this guy."

Donovan's face darkened. He didn't like being contradicted, especially when Zaren was offering him what he wanted: a chance to carry on as planned.

McKenzie looked dubiously between the captain and the screen, and for once he was on my side. "We don't know anything about these aliens, sir. Maybe we should check them out before we assume—"

"Nonsense." The captain's voice was firm, though he looked anything but certain. "They're in pursuit of a dangerous criminal, and we owe it to the galactic community to assist them. Fortunately we've already taken the fugitive into custody."

Before either of us could object, he switched back to Galtrade and addressed the alien on screen.

"Captain Zaren, I am Captain Donovan, commanding the *Wandering Star*," he said, reeling off a memorized phrase. As he started to improvise, his words became less certain. "We have your, ah, vresin? Yes. In our ship."

I winced at the sharp, merciless grin that spread across the alien's face. The ships on the screen were already starting to converge on our location. They'd started to accelerate towards the *Wandering Star* even before Captain Donovan confirmed that Auric was aboard.

Either they were sure we'd picked him up, or we'd been their destination from the start. I didn't like that thought.

"Good, good," Zaren said. "You will keep him? Until we arrive."

"Of course," Captain Donovan said, apparently oblivious to the danger. Just proud to be of service in a way that cost him nothing at all.

The alien turned and hissed something over his shoulder, switching from Galtrade to a language I didn't know. I looked at Mr. Mews, hoping that he could at least identify the language, but no. The holographic cat looked as mystified as I was.

Before we could respond, the screen went blank. Donovan sat back in his chair, looking pleased with himself. "Capital. Now we can get rid of the troublemaker and be on our way as planned. How long till they arrive, McKenzie?"

The navigator looked torn between hope that the captain was right and fear that we were welcoming a disaster in. "The closest ship will be here in... thirty-four minutes, Captain."

"Good, good. Enough time for me to get a fresh uniform on," Donovan said, then looked at me. "Tamara, you'd better make sure the deck can take a ship landing on it."

"Captain, the drones—"

"Make sure they're doing it right," he snapped, interrupting me. "I want you to check on them. Go."

You mean you want me out of your way. I didn't have much choice though; it was clear he wouldn't listen. McKenzie looked almost sympathetic when I turned to him, but he didn't speak up. Fat chance he'd back me against the captain.

Turning on my heel, I marched off the bridge and tried to think of anything I could do to protect the colonists from the disaster I felt descending on us. Thirty-four minutes wasn't long enough to do much, but it was all the time I had.

6

AURIC

I prowled around the small room, struggling to keep my emotions under control. The Silver Band might arrive at any time, and I had to be free when they got here.

I'd waited as long as my patience would allow. Longer than was safe. But still the humans kept me locked up in this tiny space filled with primitive medical equipment. This room was more comfortable than a cell, but just as secure. I cursed the ill luck that had brought me down hard enough to lose consciousness.

"Open the door," I shouted, hoping that the sound would carry through the door. I had to get the humans to understand the danger they were in or this would all be for nothing. My flight from the Silver Band, the risks I'd taken overloading the engine to get here ahead of them. All of it.

There is no point in recriminations. The voice was that

of my father, patient and firm. *You acted with honor, which is all that matters. The rest is up to fate.*

It was exactly what he'd have said if he was alive and with me. Infuriating advice that made me want to punch his ghost. What use was acting with honor if it helped no one? If the Silver Band attacked these humans, killed or enslaved them, what good had I done?

You've done your best. Damn it, I could still hear him. *Better to die doing the right thing than to prosper doing wrong.*

That had been his philosophy in life, and even in death he wouldn't shut up about it.

"Very well, Father," I said aloud, and sighed. "But better still to live doing right."

His memory had no answer to that, and I smiled sadly. I might grouse about the advice he gave me, but it was nice to hear his voice again. Even if it was just my memory of him.

"Time to get to work." I hammered my fist on the door, hoping one of the humans would respond. They had to listen. I refused to accept failure.

It took longer than I'd hoped to get a response, but eventually the screen lit up again.

"Quiet," a human snapped in accented Galtrade. She consulted a hologram at her wrist, frowned, and carefully pronounced another word. "Working."

It was the blonde human female, not the dark-haired beauty I'd hoped to see again. But at least someone was speaking to me. Perhaps she'd even listen.

"Let me out," I demanded. "You are in great danger."

I kept my language as simple as possible, but the confusion on her face told me that wasn't enough. I growled to myself, trying to hide my anger. Who would go to space not knowing Galtrade?

That was unfair, I knew. The humans were new to space, and the odds of their ship bumping into anyone on this journey were slim. They *should* have been safe without knowing the language of space.

"Danger," I tried again, keeping my frustration in check and speaking slowly. The hologram at her wrist translated for her and I hoped that she would listen. "Big danger. Open door?"

She snapped something in her own language, glaring at me, and following it with a single word of Galtrade. "Quiet."

That was one word she knew well. Unfortunately, it wasn't very helpful.

The screen went dark again, and I howled in frustration. My instincts told me that time was running out, and I had no way to save the foolish humans from their complacency. It might already be too late.

I hammered on the door again, but there was no answer. Whatever the human outside was doing, she wasn't going to listen. Not that I had any hope of convincing her across the language barrier, anyway.

Red hot rage filled me, a wave of helpless fury. Zaren

would be here soon, and then everything would be over, for me and for the humans. My rebellion would have achieved nothing aside from salving my conscience.

No. I would not let that happen. If I couldn't save all the humans, I would at least save Tamara, the beautiful engineer. There had to be a way out of this trap. Turning my attention to the rest of the room, I searched for one.

Nothing. The air vents were far too small for anyone to climb through. The food hatch too. This was some kind of isolation chamber, designed to keep me away from the rest of the humans' ship. A good plan in a lot of ways — if I'd been an enemy, this would have made an excellent prison.

I tore up the flooring, pulled panels from the wall, levered a length of metal from the bed frame and used it as a club. It didn't leave so much as a scratch on the wall. Panting, I backed away and sat amongst the wreckage of the room, trying to think of something I could do.

If nothing else, I could be ready for Zaren. When he opened the door, I'd be waiting with this crude club in hand. I might be doomed, but I could take him with me.

As though that thought had summoned him, the door slid open. I bounced to my feet instantly, crude weapon swinging up.

And stopped, frozen in place. It wasn't my nemesis standing there, or one of his soldiers. Instead, I was face to face with Tamara, her piercing green eyes wide in shock as I loomed over her.

I stepped back, dropping my improvised weapon and showing my empty hands. I could have pushed past her, freed myself — but she'd come here for a reason. Better to find out what it was.

She stayed still as a statue for a moment, only her eyes moving, darting around. Looking at the chaos I'd unleashed on the room. Her jaw tensed, her weight shifted, and I knew she was tempted to turn, run, slam the door again and leave me. I couldn't blame her. Surrounded by the wreckage of the room, I must look like an unhinged killer to her.

But she mastered her fear, pushing it down and taking a step into the room. The door slid shut behind her, locking her in with me.

What in the Starless Void was she doing? She was safe in my presence but she couldn't be sure of that. As far as she knew, I could be a deadly danger.

The human female was no fool. She knew she'd put herself in my hands, and I could see the fear in her pale face. In the way she shifted from foot to foot, ready to run though there was nowhere to go.

I sat down, the only thing I could think of to make myself less threatening. The small room didn't give us much space, and there was nowhere she could stand that would be out of my reach.

Now that there was nothing between us but air, I ached to reach out and touch her, take her. I restrained myself with difficulty. This wasn't the place, and there was no time. If the Silver Band wasn't here yet, they would arrive soon.

My body's demands would have to wait until she was safe.

"You must release me," I said, keeping my tone soft and unthreatening. "You are in great danger."

"Are you a fugitive?" she asked in return. I shook my head instinctively, then thought about it for a moment.

"Perhaps," I allowed, trying to work out how to explain my situation. Zaren would have declared me one by now.

If the humans had heard of that, it meant he was in system. Starless Void.

"Zaren is here?" I asked. "How long before he docks?"

Too much, too fast. I'd lost her. The confusion on her face made it clear she wasn't following my words. But a flash of recognition at the name 'Zaren' confirmed that he'd spoken with the humans.

I gathered myself, leaned forward and met her eyes. I had to convince her, and quickly, or we were all doomed. It might already be too late.

"We must leave. Zaren is the danger." Better. Tamara understood, but that didn't mean she'd believe me.

7

TAMARA

The alien warrior looked at me, practically vibrating with urgency. But was that because we were all in danger, or just him?

His body language told me a lot more than his words did. The tension in his shoulders, the way his eyes kept flicking to the door and back. The alien warrior was afraid, but something made me certain it wasn't for himself.

For me, perhaps, and the rest of the crew of the *Wandering Star*? I couldn't tell.

There was something else in his expression, something I didn't want to look at too closely. A hunger I didn't have time to consider now. It would only distract me if I let myself think about it, and about his perfect washboard abs, and... *Crap. Focus, Tamara!*

I needed to get more out of him, but the language barrier didn't make it easy. Okay, there were ways to work around that. I called up Mr. Mews, the hologram appearing on my wrist and hissing at Auric. The alien frowned at my companion but didn't say anything.

"Right, Mr. Mews, you're going to have to help translate," I said, hoping that the cat could handle that. He still had access to the Galtrade database, but that wasn't the same as speaking the language. That would have made things too simple.

Auric spoke again, too fast for me. Mr. Mews slowed it down, replacing some of the words with English, and left me to fill in the rest. Not great, but a start.

How long before Zaren... something. I sighed, pushed a hand through my hair, and guessed. Arrives or docks or something like that, it had to be. At this speed the conversation would take forever, and we didn't have much time.

"Not long," I answered. That much was easy. My next questions not so much. "Why is he chasing you? Are you in trouble?"

I needed Mr. Mews' help translating that, and it took a frustratingly long time to get the point across. Auric growled, pacing to and fro in the tiny room. At last I got my questions into a form he understood.

"Not chasing me," he answered through the translation. "Coming here for *you*. I arrived first, to warn you."

I blinked. "Us? What do they want with us?"

"They want all this." His sweeping gesture took in the whole of the *Wandering Star*. "So much wealth. Resources. Zaren will steal it all."

My jaw tightened and I swallowed nervously.

Reminding myself that I had no reason to trust his word over Zaren's, I tried to work out who to believe.

"Why?" I asked, hoping more information would help. Auric shrugged.

"Power. Power and strength in our..." He broke into language that I didn't follow and Mr. Mews was no help. Auric snarled, frustration showing, and punched the wall.

"Very big fight?" he tried. "Lost many ships. No planets."

I saw the desperation in his body language. The hope that I'd understand, the fear that I wouldn't. He trembled with frustration and I did my best to follow what he was telling me.

"So you're at war," I said in English. He wouldn't understand, but saying it out loud helped me think it through. "And it's costing you a lot. Lots of ships blown up. You need resources? Oh."

I thought about our cargo holds. Full of all the supplies a colony would need, enough to last thousands of people for years. Animals in suspended animation, seeds. Fuel and machinery. "You want our supplies. No, not you. Your people?"

Auric nodded, encouraging me. Did he understand? No, my words meant nothing to him. But he wanted me to figure it out. I bit my lip.

"Fine. So you came ahead to warn us because... why?" Maybe with Mr. Mews' help I could have asked him that, but it would take time. If I understood what Auric said, the *Wandering Star* was in deadly danger.

He'd taken the risk to come and warn us, his reasons didn't matter.

I reached out to take his hand, squeezing it gently. His powerful eyes met mine and I shivered at the sense of connection between us. The last bit of doubt faded as I remembered Zaren's shark-like smile.

What's the worst that can happen if I trust him? We jump early, lose a couple of weeks recharging and getting back on course. Auric escapes whatever justice is chasing him. I'll be in the shit, obviously, but all Donovan can do is chew me out. I sighed. No, if he gave me a bad enough evaluation that Arcadia wouldn't take me. They'd send me back to Earth. I could live with that if I had to.

Or he could call it mutiny and space me. Yeah, that didn't sound great.

But the alternative was unthinkable. If Zaren and the other aliens attacked and seized the *Wandering Star*, there was no telling what would happen to us. Or to the thousands of colonists in cold storage. The only options there were bad — either we'd have no value to the attackers, in which case they'd dump us into space to die. Or we *would* have value. As slaves, maybe, or food.

I pictured Zaren's smile, those sharp teeth, and shuddered. Surely his people wouldn't eat humans?

It doesn't matter, I told myself. *Either we'll die or we'll live as slaves, and that's not something I can let happen.*

"Okay," I said in Galtrade. "I believe you. But I cannot move the ship on my own."

It had to be possible to jump early or there wouldn't

be warnings against it. I just didn't know how. I might be able to override the engine's safety features, but someone else had to fly the ship.

Donovan had made it clear he wouldn't do it. McKenzie might be more dubious about the incoming ships, but enough to disobey the captain? I doubted it.

"I am pilot," Auric said as though he'd read my mind. An irrational panic flooded through me — was he psychic? If so, did that mean he saw what I thought when I looked at him?

Great, Tamara. Way to focus on what matters. Anyway, he didn't need to read my mind. Auric knew I was an engineer, and he could put two and two together. If I needed help, it would be from someone who could fly the ship.

He couldn't see the images that leaped into my mind every time I looked at his muscular body. The thoughts of him sweeping me into his arms, pulling me to him, his lips on mine... *God damn it, Tamara, focus!*

"I will get ship ready," I said, shaking off those fantasies and hoping he'd understand what I meant. He nodded. "But we can't go. Not until we are sure."

I guess I'm doing this. Crap. I wasn't exactly comfortable with the idea of committing mutiny, but the alternative was even worse. I was fairly confident that Captain Donovan wouldn't space me for it, anyway. Lock me up till we reached Arcadia? Sure.

Maybe, if I was lucky, I'd be locked up with Auric.

Annoyed at myself, I tried to focus. Auric didn't make it easy. He was gorgeous, with a body to stop anyone from thinking straight. Worse, he knew how good he looked — there was no self-consciousness to him as he caught me looking.

Face flushed, I pried my gaze away. We needed to get out of here, and thinking about jumping him was a distraction I couldn't afford.

The sickbay was still empty, thank god. Dr. Orson had only stepped out to get some food, and we had to be gone before she came back. Auric cast a longing glance at his weapons as we passed them, but I shook my head and pushed him past. No way was I arming him. Releasing him from his prison was enough of a risk.

He could have brushed me aside and taken the weapons. Now that I'd let him out of his makeshift cell I had no way to control him. For a moment I worried that I'd made a terrible mistake but Auric let me push him away from the weapons and out into the corridor.

From my wrist, Mr. Mews trilled a message alert. I cursed under my breath and looked at it. Not good news — the first alien ship was nearly here, and the captain wanted to know if the deck was safe to land on.

That had never been in question — the damage had been superficial and easy for drones to repair. But I didn't want to encourage Zaren and co. to land at all. I sent a quick response.

> INTERNAL DAMAGE STILL BEING CHECKED. WILL BE DONE SOON! CAN'T GUARANTEE SAFETY YET.

There. Hopefully that would delay them long enough for us to reach the engine room. Mr. Mews trilled again, the hologram cat looking smug as the captain's reply appeared over his head.

GET IT DONE. I WILL NOT RISK A DIPLOMATIC INCIDENT. REPORT IN 10 MINS.

Great. A time limit. Just what I need. Setting a timer so I wouldn't forget to send a fake 'update' on the repairs, I turned to Auric.

"They're here," I told him. He nodded, a grim snarl showing before he controlled his features. Gesturing for me to lead the way, he looked ready for a fight. I hoped it wouldn't come to that.

I set off at a jog. Ten minutes gave us more than enough time to make it to engineering by the most direct route, but that also took us across the open deck. Sticking to the corridors where we'd be safely out of sight would take longer — too long.

We had to chance the deck.

Mr. Mews meowed for attention again and I brushed him off. I had nothing to say to the captain and stopping to say it would only waste time we didn't have. The doors to the upper deck were just ahead — a quick dash across and we'd be at the stairs down to the engine room.

I opened the doors and froze, Auric almost running into me. Mr. Mews looked up as though to say he'd tried to warn me.

Another alien ship hung in the air above the deck, coming in to land. Damn it. Why had I ever thought the aliens would listen to my warnings? If Donovan had even tried to tell them to stop, the aliens must have ignored him. I backed away quickly, getting out of sight before anyone emerged.

"What do I do now?" I asked Mr. Mews, who just looked up at me with his big eyes. It wasn't fair to expect the hologram to suggest something, but then it wasn't fair to ask me to deal with this either.

We couldn't get past them. As soon as we stepped out of the door, they'd see us. But heading back below decks and going the long way through the warren of corridors would take too long. What was the point? Now that the aliens were aboard I had no chance of convincing the captain to jump the ship.

Auric would have to seize control of the bridge by force. I winced at the idea. Was I seriously considering helping an alien pirate take the *Wandering Star?*

I wished I knew how to ask his advice, but it was impossible. Even trying to phrase the question in Galtrade gave me a headache. I gritted my teeth and turned back to the doorway, peering around it and hoping for inspiration to strike.

The alien ship descended smoothly. Unlike Auric's craft, this one came in slow and gentle, landing with a majestic grace that belied its bulk. No one-person fighter, this ship was the size of a small truck.

Donovan marched out from the bridge, accompanied by Maxwell with his rifle. I sighed with relief — at least he'd taken the minimal precaution of bringing an armed guard along. A glance at Auric killed that relief though. If he was typical of his kind, then Maxwell wouldn't stand a chance.

All I could do was watch and hope. Auric stood close behind me, his presence a comfort and a distraction as we waited for a chance to move.

A ramp lowered from the spaceship, clanging to the *Wandering Star's* deck, and out came three prytheen warriors. Each of the blue-skinned aliens had to be over six foot tall, and they wore black uniforms that clung to their muscular bodies.

I guess Auric isn't the only impressive specimen among these aliens. None of them looked quite as powerful as he did, but they were all armed and dangerous.

Donovan adjusted his jacket and stepped forward, doing his best to hide his nerves and failing. He extended a hand in greeting, cleared his throat and spoke.

"Friends," he said, his accented Galtrade sounding awful even to my ears. At least he'd made an effort and practiced what he wanted to say. "Welcome aboard the *Wandering Star.*"

The aliens looked at each other, and even from this distance I saw the cruel amusement in their smiles. Without even bothering to answer, the leader drew a pistol and fired it point-blank into Captain Donovan's chest.

8

AURIC

Tamara drew breath for a scream, and I grabbed her before she could give away our location. Outside, the body of the human captain toppled in slow motion, falling to the ground as I pulled Tamara back out of sight. My hand covered her mouth, muffling the sounds she made.

Instead of screaming, she bit me. Teeth sank into my palm, hard and deep, and now I was the one struggling to keep quiet. I had an armful of a feral human, biting and clawing at me.

Outside, another blaster shot echoed. The remaining human screamed and fell silent. The humans were no match for trained prytheen warriors, especially not when outnumbered and taken by surprise.

"Sundered *Space,* woman, stop that," I hissed in her ear. "I'm trying to save your life!"

If the human female understood a word I said, she didn't care. Biting harder, she stomped down on my foot and I bit back a frustrated roar as we struggled in the small space.

Winning would have been easy if I'd been willing to hurt her, but I wasn't. I couldn't. Cursing my instincts I pushed her against the wall, pinning her with my weight and trapping her as best I could.

She thrashed in my grip, and I was hyper-aware of her squirming body against mine. Even now I couldn't help responding to it, to her.

"Quiet," I said, keeping my words simple. "You must be quiet."

Thank the blessed ones, she understood. Or at least, she fell silent and stopped struggling. Cautiously, I removed my hand from her mouth.

No scream. Good. Hopefully the noise we'd made in our little struggle hadn't attracted any attention. Stepping back and letting her down, I braced myself for a renewed fight.

Fortunately for us both, Tamara was smarter than that. Steadying herself against the wall, face pale, she made no move to fight me or to scream. I hoped that meant that she knew I was on her side.

She whispered something in her own language. The words meant nothing to me, of course, but I could feel her horror and disgust.

I shared it. The 'warrior' out there didn't deserve the title: gunning down the captain of this ship without warning or hesitation was an act without honor.

At least only one ship has arrived. Three prytheen warriors aboard the *Wandering Star* was a bad start, but if more arrived it would be impossible to keep the humans safe.

Three would be more than enough to seize the humans' ship and hold it. The rest of the Silver Band would be on us soon, too soon, and we needed to leave before they arrived.

Risking a look out of the doorway I saw that the second human still lived. The battle was over, though, and that was no surprise: the humans hadn't been ready for a fight.

Standing over the body of the captain, the living human dangling from his grip, a prytheen warrior laughed. I recognized him — Kozan, a hero of Zaren's campaigns.

I wasn't sure whether that made the human luckier than his comrades or not. Yes, he was alive, but he might come to regret that. Kozan was Zaren's creature, and that meant I couldn't expect him to treat a captive honorably.

"Where is Auric?" Kozan demanded in Galtrade, and I cursed under my breath. Of course they'd want to make sure I was secure.

The human stared at his captor, uncomprehending. Kozan had to repeat the question twice before it sank in and the human pointed in the direction of the sickbay.

Great. They're coming this way.

"Go," I told Tamara, stepping back and pointing

into the ship. "I will stop them."

Tamara turned to look at me. Said something incomprehensible in her own language. A warning, I thought, or perhaps a blessing. There was no way to be sure. What was clear was that she was worried.

Not about what I would do, but whether I would survive it.

I smiled a hungry smile, and pushed her on her way. A fight while outnumbered three to one wasn't a good idea, but at least this was a danger I'd prepared for all my life. A simple challenge, one where I knew what I was doing.

Tamara put a hand on my back, a brief contact that sent a wave of warmth through me. Her support meant more to me than I could tell her, but right now I needed her to *go*. If she got caught in the fight that was about to erupt I wouldn't forgive myself.

Before I could say anything, she retreated into the corridors from which we'd come. Hopefully to find another way to the engine room, but as long as she was safe from the fight, that would do.

Kozan shoved his human captive through the doorway ahead of him. Exactly as I'd expected — I grabbed the human and pulled him past me, sending him tumbling into the ship as I met Kozan's surprised glare.

I couldn't give him time to recover. He was armed and had backup while I had nothing, no weapons or allies. This first moment of shock was my only chance.

My punch struck Kozan in the throat, sending him

staggering back gasping for air. He collided with the warrior behind him and the two of them tangled each other.

I followed up, fast and hard. There was no time for subtle tricks or clever feints — if either of two managed to draw a weapon, I didn't stand a chance. Grabbing Kozan's wrist as he tried to pull his pistol, I snatched a knife from his belt and slashed at his companion's throat.

The blade bit deep, sending the man back in a spray of blood. For a moment, I regretted that. I didn't know this warrior, who he was or why he was here. I'd just snuffed out his life without knowing anything about it.

He came here to kill and steal from a weaker race, I reminded myself. *And he did nothing to stop Kozan from shooting the human captain. I have nothing to be ashamed of.*

But my moment of hesitation gave Kozan time to recover, to pull his arm free of my grip and dive away. I swung the blade, catching him with a shallow cut that barely drew blood, and then he had his blaster out.

I hit the deck and a beam of plasma seared over me, heat scorching my back. Rolling desperately aside, I barely avoided his second shot. He took aim as I leaped up, and I knew that his third shot would finish me unless I did something unexpected.

The knife wasn't balanced for throwing but I tried anyway. Kozan dodged, the movement putting his aim off center, and the beam missed me by a finger-width. I felt the heat wash over me as I leaped toward him, one hand closing on his forearm and the other grabbing at his throat.

His knee came up hard, and I twisted to take the blow on my hip. Locked together, we tumbled to the deck, rolling over and over as we fought for control of the blaster. Energy bolts went wild, the heat burning both of us, and neither of us could get an advantage.

Where's the third warrior? I hadn't seen him when the door opened, and now I had no time to look for him. My shoulder blades itched — if he came up behind me, it was all over. I had to win this fight, fast.

Headbutting Kozan as hard as I could, I drove him back down into the decking. Grabbing his blaster pistol in both hands, I forced it down into Kozan's chest and squeezed the trigger.

At point-blank range, the energy bolt tore straight through him and the deck below. The Silver Band commander bucked and stopped moving as I let go of the blaster with a wince. My hands burned where I'd held the barrel, but the fight was over.

I looked up at the sky through the forcefield. No other ships were close enough to see, but they'd arrive too soon for comfort. The Silver Band was on its way.

If the humans didn't get their ship out of this system, everything was lost. And somewhere on the *Wandering Star* was the third prytheen warrior, working to stop anyone interfering with the attack. He'd head for the engine room or the bridge, and I could only get to one of them.

The choice was easy to make. Tamara would be in

the engine room, and if he caught her there... I couldn't finish the thought, but an angry snarl spread across my face.

I had to find him before it was too late.

9

TAMARA

My communicator lit up as I ran, messages from McKenzie flooding it. Mr. Mews kept trying to tell me I had urgent notifications, and I wished there was a way to shut him up.

I know! The captain's dead, the ship's under attack. Everything's going wrong. What more is there to say? Worst of all, I had no idea how the fight behind me was going. Auric had seemed confident when he pushed me back into the ship, but he was up against three fully-armed enemies. And he'd just lived through a crash.

Against odds like that I had to assume he'd lose. If I was lucky, he'd take some of the enemy with him, but I couldn't count on it. I swallowed painfully, images of him lying dead on the deck coming to mind unbidden.

Why did that hurt so much?

The idea of Auric dead felt worse than Donovan being killed. Okay, I hadn't *liked* Donovan, but he was my boss and I'd known him for months. Auric? We'd just met, but the image of him dying left a cold weight in my heart.

Don't think about it, just run, I told myself, panting as I made my way through the corridors. I hadn't run this fast in months — it turned out that being chased by murderous aliens was a great motivator.

Bursting into the engine room, I slammed the door behind me and leaned against the wall panting. My muscles ached and my side hurt from running, but I was safe. Well, safe-ish. I doubted those alien blaster pistols would take long to burn through the door.

Don't borrow trouble, things are bad enough. I forced my eyes open and looked at the hyperdrive that filled most of the room. Plastered with warning stickers, almost all of the controls were off-limits. Or they were supposed to be. Right now I wouldn't let the rules stand in my way.

Mr. Mews still yowled for my attention, and as I tore the stickers out of the way, I told him to put the call through. Getting the engine ready wasn't enough on its own, I needed a pilot.

"Where have you been?" McKenzie shouted into the comm as soon as the call connected. Mr. Mews hissed, not liking his tone. I wrenched open an inspection hatch, grabbing my tools and getting to work.

"Running to engineering," I shouted back as I tried to find the overrides that would let the drive operate at less than full power. "Are you on the bridge?"

"Those alien bastards killed the captain," he said, ignoring my question. "They're going to kill us all."

"I know, I saw it. McKenzie, *are you on the bridge?* We have to jump the ship before the rest of them get here."

"Yes," he stammered. "I'm here. I locked the doors when I saw them kill the captain. I... oh god."

Finally he shut up for a second. I heard him breathing heavily, panting almost, trying to get his panic under control. Giving him a chance to get himself together, I worked fast. Praying I wouldn't damage anything important, I made my best guesses at what I needed to patch.

An engineer shouldn't work on guesses, my father would have told me. But today I had no choice.

"We can't," he answered at last. "We can't reach the next stop, Tamara, we're all going to die."

"Don't worry about the engines, I can get them to behave," I told him, trying to sound more confident than I felt. If we stayed here we stood no chance at all. "You just need to plot a course. Do you want to be here when the rest of the aliens arrive?"

"Fuck no," McKenzie said. "But we can't jump, not for days. We've got to surrender, right? What choice do we have?"

"We can leave as soon as I short out the safeties." *And void every warranty on the ship.* My fingers trembled as I pushed a wrench across the gap where a fuse ought to go. This wasn't even slightly safe, but what choice did I have? "We've got to risk it."

"The akedians—"

"They leased us a pile of junk," I snapped, interrupting him. "Don't listen to what they say it can and can't do."

His silence filled the channel. McKenzie wasn't a brave man, and he wasn't one for bold action. Before, I'd been grateful for that: it had kept him from pushing me too far when the captain wouldn't back him up.

Now it might get us all killed. I swore under my breath.

"Look, if those aliens get aboard, we're all dead, right?" I tried. No answer. Reason wasn't working on him, not now. His panic overwhelmed it and I needed something equally scary to get through to him.

Only one thing came to mind. "Fine. I'm going to jump the ship as soon as I can. If we don't have a new course laid in, we'll come out in deep space, too far from a star to recharge the engines. Understand?"

McKenzie gasped. Every spacer had nightmares about being lost in the dark between the stars. The supplies on this ship would last a long time, but there'd be no resupply and no way for rescue to find us. Death would come for us slowly in the dark between the stars.

"You can't do that," he protested. "You'll kill us all."

"It's me or those aliens," I told him, getting back to work. "Or you can set a course to a star we can reach, and we'll live."

Frantic typing answered me and I grinned. A small victory, but I'd gotten what I wanted. He was setting a course.

"This is insane," he complained as he worked. "It

takes hours to plot a safe course. You can't expect me to get this done in minutes."

"Just do your best," I encouraged him. It wasn't as though we had any choice, and the course didn't have to be perfect. As long as we didn't come out right on top of something, we'd be okay. I hoped.

Behind me, something heavy slammed into the door. I winced and looked up at the sound. "They've found me."

McKenzie started to say something but I killed the connection. Let him take the time to set it up again, I had a better use for the communicator right now.

"Mr. Mews, show me the security footage from outside the engine room," I said. The holographic cat purred an acknowledgement and a grainy image appeared beside him. A blue skinned alien hammering on the heavy door with his fists.

For a moment my heart leaped and I hoped it was Auric. But no, that was wishful thinking. Auric hadn't worn that black uniform. It was one of the attackers, coming to stop our escape. As I watched, the alien drew his pistol and fired a beam into the door, starting to cut his way through.

My heart froze, the last hope that Auric was alive draining away. I wiped unexpected tears from my eyes and turned back to my work. If Auric had died fighting for me, I wouldn't waste his sacrifice.

At least there's only one alien out there, I told myself. Maybe Auric had killed the others. That evened the odds and gave us a fighting chance, but it was still

Orson, McKenzie and me against a trained alien warrior. Not exactly heartening, even if the rest of the plan worked perfectly.

I looked at the mess I'd made of the drive. The vast energies that the ship had built up were going into motion now, ready to rip a hole in space and push the *Wandering Star* through it. Hopefully it would work, and not kill us all.

It would still be minutes before the drive fired — minutes in which the alien could cancel the jump. The door glowed where the beam struck it and I knew I wouldn't have that long. The alien weapon cut through the steel with terrible efficiency.

I picked up my heaviest wrench and stood against the wall beside the door. After my brief struggle with Auric, I doubted I'd be able to win a fight against one of these aliens, but I knew for sure that I wasn't going to give up without trying. *All I need to do is slow him down until we jump.*

The glowing patch on the door spread as the alien's blaster cut through the hinges, and my heart hammered in my chest. I tried not to think about Auric's fate. Was he lying somewhere, dead or dying? No good could come of thinking about that. The wrench felt slippery in my hands as I raised it high.

I might not be much of a fighter, but I'd do my best to avenge Auric.

The heavy door rang like a bell as the alien warrior kicked it open, and he pounced through the opening like a tiger. I swung the wrench down with all my strength, feeling the shudder of impact as it struck the man's wrist. The ugly snap of breaking bone filled the room and his pistol went flying into the depths of the engine room.

That was my first and only piece of good luck. Before I could pull the wrench back for a second blow, he was on me. His left hand slammed into my stomach hard, driving all the air from me and throwing me back against the wall. I didn't even see the next punch coming, it was so fast, and it rocked my head to the side leaving me seeing stars. Everything seemed to move in slow motion as I slid down the cold metal wall.

I tried to raise the wrench, but my grip was too weak. The alien plucked it from my hand easily and threw it aside with a look of contempt.

He growled something in a language I didn't understand, but I recognized an insult when I heard one. And a threat. Pinning me against the wall, he grinned, sharp teeth glinting in the light. Out of other ideas, I did the only thing I could think of and brought my knee up as hard as possible between his legs.

If he'd been paying any attention at all it wouldn't have worked, but he underestimated me again. Gasping and staggering back, my attacker gave me just enough space to leap away. I dove for the floor, looking for the pistol he'd dropped. His good hand caught my leg as I scrabbled desperately, trying to find the only weapon that would give me a chance.

There! The pistol lay under the drive casing, almost

in reach. Almost but not quite. The alien's hand closed on my ankle, pulling me back, and my fingers missed the weapon by inches.

I tried to kick back at his face but he just laughed, dragging me out into the open. My only chance slipped out of reach.

He hissed something awful-sounding and grabbed at my belt. I didn't want to find out what he had in mind for me, but even with an injured wrist he was more than capable of pinning me. I looked up at him, panic setting in as he pulled a knife from his belt.

This is it, I thought. I'd failed. Failed to avenge Auric, failed to jump the ship to safety. Failed to achieve anything. I was going to die here at the knife of this monstrous alien warrior, and there was nothing I could do about it.

The alien warrior looked down at me, savoring my defeat and enjoying my fear. He traced the tip of his blade down my neck, pressing just hard enough to hurt without breaking the skin. It looked like he wanted to enjoy my suffering after the pain I'd visited on him.

"Tresh prensec chro," he said. I didn't know what that meant, and I didn't think I wanted to.

"Get on with it," I spat back at him, refusing to let him see how frightened I was. "Come on, do it!"

His nasty smile widened and he raised the blade. I saw it gleam in the lights, strangely beautiful for something that was about to kill me. My eyes locked on it, watching the blade rise.

Pause.

I took what I expected to be my last breath, and then the alien's head exploded. A light as bright as the sun tore through him, and his headless body spasmed, falling to the floor in a shower of blood. The knife came down towards me, carried by his weight, and all I could do was watch as it swung towards me. Missed me by an inch. Clanged into the decking beside my neck.

I blinked, sucking in a shaking breath, surprised I was still alive. The alien's weight trapped me and I couldn't see my savior, but I knew who it was. Who it had to be.

As Auric hauled the corpse off me, throwing him aside with casual strength, I breathed a sigh of relief for both of us. His concerned gaze raked across my body, checking for injuries before he relaxed and offered me a hand.

"You took your sweet time getting here," I said in English, knowing he wouldn't understand. It was an ungrateful sentiment but I needed to let out some of my frustration.

I took his hand and he hauled me up with no difficulty at all.

"Must leave now," he said in Galtrade, holding up an alien communicator flickering with information. "Too many close ships."

The display meant nothing to me but I trusted he knew what he was talking about. If the alien ships got too close, they would get sucked into the drive field — the quicker I hit the switch, the more likely we were to escape on our own.

McKenzie's had plenty of time to set a course, I thought as I ran to the control panel. Half the warning lights were amber, several more were red, and as I uncovered the warp switch an alarm blared. The akedians were *serious* about us not using the drive this way.

Tough. I brought my hand down on the switch with as much force as I had.

The universe disappeared around me as we made our jump.

10

AURIC

*A*larms blared as the universe sprang back into existence. Sparks showered the engine room from Tamara's improvised overrides and flames leaped from the panels, lighting the room in a ruddy glow.

Which was useful, because all the lights were out. The jump had used every bit of stored energy the human ship had — the question was, had we reached a destination where we could survive?

And would the Silver Band follow?

There wasn't time to worry about that now. Flames threatened to engulf us and the entire ship shook as the pilot tried to maneuver.

"We must leave," I said to Tamara, who was staring in horror at the damage she'd done to her own engine room. The fire spread fast, whatever fire suppression systems the ship had were not kicking in.

Tamara nodded, my words snapping her out of her paralysis. Grabbing my arm, she pulled me out through the ruined door and out of the flame-lit chamber. Smoke billowed around us and she staggered, coughing and choking.

I didn't hesitate, picking her up and throwing her over my shoulder. Long strides took us up towards the deck, but as we passed the next door Tamara pounded on my back.

"Wait," she shouted, coughing. My instincts screamed at me to get her up, out of the smoke and away from the fire, but I put her down and hoped she knew what she was doing.

Pulling open a red hatch on the wall, Tamara pulled a lever inside. Instantly a door slammed down between us and the fire and I felt the ship shudder.

"Vacuum," Tamara gasped, leaning against the wall to catch her breath. "Let the air out…"

She trailed off in coughs again, but I understood. The emergency system would vent the air out from the burning area and starve the flames. Primitive but effective, though it would have killed anyone trapped inside.

Before we had a chance to say more, the ship shuddered under us. Something was wrong, something more than the fire. I had to know what. Taking Tamara by the arm, I pulled her with me as I ran out onto the deck.

And stopped, awed by the sight that greeted us. Above us, the sky wheeled too quickly, and a planet filled half of it. The *Wandering Star* had come out of hyperspace far too close, and we were falling fast. I hoped the human on the bridge managed to bring the ship under control. If he didn't, the ship would plunge to its destruction and all of this would have been for nothing.

The artificial gravity shuddered, and for a moment I thought we would drift free of the deck, falling up towards the planet. Then I fell back, stumbling as the deck twisted and bucked beneath us. The ship's drive fought against the planet's gravity, trying to pull free, and it wasn't having an easy time. Above our heads the forcefield shimmered, weakening and looking like it might fail at any moment.

My teeth ground together. Death was coming for us in a dozen ways, despite everything Tamara and I had done. Were these humans cursed, doomed to die no matter what I tried?

No. I will not accept that. I can save at least one of them. Tamara yelped something as I dragged her towards Kozan's ship and carried her inside, slamming the airlock behind us. Putting the human female down in the copilot's seat, I turned to the control board.

"What are you doing?" Tamara demanded, remembering her Galtrade. She tried to stand, the seat's protective forcefield keeping her pinned in place.

"Saving you," I snapped back. "Your pilot will either get control or he will not, there is nothing more we can do to help."

I started the engines as I spoke, glad that Kozan had left his raider ready to launch at a moment's notice. Before Tamara voiced another complaint I hit the throttle, launching us into space and pulling away from the *Wandering Star*.

Hopefully the humans would make it to the planet's surface, but if not, at least Tamara would be safe. I would have something to show for my actions.

The planet was too close above. Green and blue and white, the colors of life — which was good news and bad. The *Wandering Star* was tumbling down towards it and I doubted the humans would pull up in time, so it was good that they'd be able to survive on the surface. But it also meant the Tavesh Empire might care about this world.

My stolen heavy raider accelerated slowly compared to the agile fighter I preferred to fly, but this was what I had.

Beside me, Tamara struggled against the forcefield. Not wanting to deal with a panicking human and flying the ship, I dialed up the field to maximum strength. That would be difficult for a prytheen to fight free of, and Tamara fell back into the chair with a gasp as it gripped her.

We pulled away from the planet and I caught my breath as the raider steadied itself. We were going to make it clear of the gravity well. At least one human would survive this mess.

"Where are we going?" Tamara gasped from her seat beside me.

"To safety," I replied. "I can save you at least."

She gasped something I didn't understand and lay back in the chair. I glanced over, caught between bitter amusement and worry for her safety. I'd killed three prytheen warriors for her and she didn't care.

And why does that matter? I didn't do it for her thanks, I did it for my own honor. I shrugged uncomfortably, trying to keep control of my emotions. For the first time since we'd met I didn't have the pressure of imminent death hanging over us both and I could afford a moment to think about other things.

Like just how beautiful the human female was. Had I really just thrown her into this raider to get her away from danger, or did I want her to myself for other reasons?

I shook my head to clear it, focusing on the displays. We had enough charge for a jump, thank the blessed stars. If I chose, we could leave this place behind. But that would mean abandoning the *Wandering Star* to its fate, along with Tamara's people.

They might not be savable anyway. The fire damage and Tamara's hasty fixes had left the hyperdrive a mess — perhaps their best hope was us fetching help? But who would dare cross the borders of the Tavesh Empire in search of a lost colony ship? Better, much better, if the ship left on its own, quietly and without being noticed.

Which would mean bringing Tamara back to repair the damage.

I looked at the sensors. Behind us, the *Wandering Star* was wreathed in flames as it descended into the atmosphere. It looked like it was coming apart, but no. The bits were too big, and their paths too deliberate.

The human ship launched its colony pods, scattering them across the planet as it went down.

"What does your captain think he's doing?" I asked.

"The captain's *dead*," Tamara shot back. "McKenzie is doing what he has to. He's trying to land, and that means dropping the pods first."

My jaw tightened, but I didn't argue. So much for leaving quietly — even under the best circumstances, it would take a long time to gather all those colonists together again. This disaster kept getting worse.

As though to prove that point, the raider's sensors started screaming warnings at me. More ships emerged from hyperspace, appearing almost on top of us. First one, then another, then a whole fleet blinking into existence exactly where the *Wandering Star* had been when it emerged. All of them caught in the gravity well of the planet below, tumbling out of formation as they struggled to adjust.

The Silver Band was here, weapons armed and ready for a fight.

I cursed under my breath. Zaren had followed after all, risking the wrath of the taveshi to claim his prize. And he'd followed the human ship's course exactly, bringing everyone who followed him out far too close to react.

My blood froze as I saw ships fall into the atmosphere and break up, howls of outrage and fear echoing from the communicator. Others managed to pull up, nearly colliding with each other as the formation dissolved into chaos.

"Kozan," Zaren's voice barked from the comms. "Kozan, what happened? Why did you let them jump?"

My lips pulled back from my teeth. Zaren had no idea that I was flying this ship, and that gave me a chance to get close. A chance I'd never have if he recognized my voice, so I stayed silent as I pulled the raider around towards his fleet.

There was no choice, not if I wanted to protect the humans. The *Wandering Star* was steadying, coming in for a rough landing, and they might make it down in one piece if I could keep the remains of Zaren's forces from interfering.

I should have known Zaren wouldn't back off. He might be dishonorable but he was no coward — and if he turned back now, he'd have broken the Code for no gain. That would be a blow he couldn't recover from. He needed something to call a victory.

And I would have to deny him that.

One pass, I told myself, looking at Tamara beside me. I'd thought this would be the safest place for her, but now it seemed that she'd have been safer back on the *Wandering Star*.

One pass, and then we jump to safety.

With luck, the Silver Band would follow me rather than the humans, if I made enough noise. I needed all attention on me, but that wouldn't be a problem.

I was close enough, in amongst the fleet. A difficult target for them all to turn on. Time to drop the ruse.

"Zaren," I shouted into the comms, arming the raider's blasters and powering up the shields to full strength. "Zaren, I challenge. You have broken the Code and are not worthy to be Alpha-Captain."

A moment's silence answered that as every warrior in the fleet heard my announcement. Then Zaren answered with a laugh.

"Auric, you are the one who defies the Council," he said. "You have no honor, and you are no part of the Silver Band. Kill him!"

A fight between alphas was a rare thing, and not a good one. Traditionally it was fought empty-handed, a warrior's claws and strength and skill tested against his foe. As I'd expected, Zaren didn't intend to honor tradition unless he had to.

One of the nearby fighters fired at me without hesitation. I dodged, firing back, blaster bolts chewing through empty space as we both maneuvered.

A fighter flew into my crosshairs and I fired, blasters ripping through its shields and hull. A bright explosion lit the sky and I winced. These warriors were my people too, and I had to remember that they had chosen to attack the innocent humans.

Other ships angled towards me, but all of us were too close to the planet's gravity well to maneuver freely. Some tumbled into the atmosphere, others struggled to avoid that fate. I drew back my lips in a hungry snarl, aiming for deep space on the far side of the fleet.

I'll draw them off and then jump, I told myself. Getting Tamara to safety was my priority, but I had to get through the fleet first. On the way past I'd take a shot at Zaren.

His fighter angled towards me, shots zipping past. All around us the sky burned with weapons fire, unimaginable destructive energies unleashed. The entire fleet targeted me.

But I was amongst them, and that made hitting me hard. None of them dared risk a shot that might hit another of the Band, so I danced my raider closer and closer to the other ships, counting on that to protect me.

My own shots hunted Zaren, but his fighter was too nimble. Blast after blast scored his shields without hitting. Soon we'd be past each other and I'd lose this chance to kill him.

The communicator crackled and spoke again, this time in Galtrade. Cold, mechanical, calm and formal.

"You are in violation of Taveshi Imperial space," the voice said. "Withdraw now or be disabled. This is your only warning."

I snarled, blood heating. That wasn't just a threat to me, but to Tamara as well. And I *would not* allow anything to happen to her while she was under my protection.

A glance at the scanners showed no sign of the taveshi ships, though, and the call was automated. There was no one to argue with, no one to fight. I concentrated on Zaren, crosshairs hunting him. Nearly...

"Warning," the communicator said again, the

accentless Galtrade of the taveshi defense system calm and cold. "Power down your weapons. Do not attempt hostilities or your vessel will be disabled."

I squeezed the trigger, firing a bolt of energy that struck the wing of Zaren's fighter and sent him into a spiral. Out of control, easy prey. I had him.

And then the taveshi defenses decided enough was enough.

With a suddenness that shocked me, the raider's power stores died. Controls dead and shields failed, leaving us defenseless and drifting. I expected to die in that moment, for one of the dozens of ships hunting us to take a killing shot. But no.

All around us, ships tumbled aimlessly through the void. Whatever weapon the taveshi had used, it had struck us all. As I watched, two fighters collided in eerie silence in front of us. Tamara gasped at the sight.

"What's going on?" Her voice was breathless, frightened, and I wanted more than anything to comfort her. But before I could speak, emergency power kicked in and I had my hands full trying to control the raider.

There wasn't enough power to escape the pull of the planet below. Gravity had a hold on us again, and on all the other prytheen ships too. We tumbled downward, and it took all my skill to avoid hitting the other ships.

"Be calm," I told the human in Galtrade. "I still have flight control."

A slight exaggeration. The ship fought me as I tried to angle us for a safe descent into the atmosphere, and a glance at the power gauges showed that the emergency batteries were draining fast. This accursed taveshi weapon might kill us yet.

Forcefields flickered around some of the raiders as they diverted power to drives and tried to pull up. An understandable mistake but a fatal one: with their power stores drained they had no way to jump to safety. Anyone who didn't make it down to the planet would die when their air scrubbers failed.

I angled downward, swearing as I struggled to control the ship. A proper landing was out of the question. I'd settle for a crash that let us survive the impact.

The air thickened around the ship as we descended, glowing red on the forcefield. I angled us for as shallow an entry as possible, giving us time to slow on the way down to the surface. It was nearly impossible to see where we were going, even the sensors were blind through the flames, so I made my best guess and prayed.

My focus was complete, it had to be. The ship only responded sluggishly to my commands and it lacked the thrust to leave the atmosphere. Around us, other ships fell, some recovering but others hitting hard. Mountains whipped past below, and then forests.

No good. Crashing amongst the trees would kill us for sure. I pulled up hard, trying to get a little more height out of the damaged ship. The emergency batteries weren't meant for this and I was running out of power fast.

I wonder how many warriors have crashed two ships in a

single day, I thought as I struggled to keep above the treetops. *Can't be many. Maybe I'm setting a record?*

There! The forest opened up ahead and I saw a lake. That gave us a chance of survival — a bad place to crash but better than hitting the trees. Fate wouldn't offer me a better landing site. I aimed for the lake and cut the power, redirecting everything I could to the forcefield that held Tamara in her chair. If I could keep her alive through the crash, I'd count it as a win whether I lived or died.

That thought filled my mind as the water struck. Then darkness.

11

TAMARA

*E*verything looked wrong and it took a moment to work out why. The ship was on its right side, and water poured in through cracks in the windshield. Cracks that were widening by the second.

Great. We're sinking.

"Auric? Auric, are you okay?" My voice sounded distant, dazed. I must have blacked out for a few seconds as we hit the water, and the impact had left me foggy. I was better off than Auric, though. The alien didn't answer, hanging in his seat to my left. Unconscious or dead, I couldn't tell.

And I didn't know which to hope for. Sure, he'd defended me against the other aliens, but they'd said they came hunting him. Had he brought this disaster on us? Or was he trying to protect us from something that would have happened anyway?

Thinking about it isn't going to get me to safety, I told

myself as I struggled to get out of the unfamiliar chair. A forcefield held me in place, making every movement an effort, and a bone-deep ache settled into me as I tried to pull free. No luck. The field gripping me would have pinned someone twice my strength.

There had to be some way to get out. Otherwise I'd drown here, and what the hell kind of safety feature was that? I fumbled at the side of the chair, fingers clumsily searching for a button, a lever, *anything* that might be a control.

Sparks flew as the water got into the ship's systems, and most of the lights went out. Water dripped onto my face. Was it my imagination or were the drops coming faster and faster?

In the darkness I saw a button glowing dimly on the panel in front of me. The emergency release? I hoped not, because I had no chance of reaching it. The forcefield kept my hands pinned to the arms of the chair.

A sudden hiss startled me, Mr. Mews announcing his displeasure at the water. I shot him a hard look.

"I don't know what you're complaining about," I told him sharply. "You're just a hologram, you can't drown."

Unless water gets into your circuitry, I reminded myself. The wristband that generated the hologram was meant to be waterproof, but I didn't exactly trust the lowest bidding company that had manufactured it. Mr. Mews stared at me, his translucent form almost invisible in the dark, and then head butted me gently. I blinked. He wasn't pinned by the forcefield — he didn't even really exist.

"Mr. Mews, I need you to do something for me," I said, slowly and carefully. He looked at me, purring agreement, and I tried to nod towards the glowing button. "Press that for me please?"

I swallowed my nerves. This wasn't what the hologram was for, and I didn't even know if the tiny forcefield could exert enough pressure to press a button. But I had to try. It was that or drown.

The virtual cat looked at me, then around at the button. Hesitated. Meowed.

"Come on," I said, trying to sound encouraging. He didn't move. "Please?"

What can I use to bribe a cat that doesn't exist? I shook my head. Stupid. Thinking about it wrong.

"You have to press it," I said, trying to sound firm. "Otherwise I'll drown. You're meant to protect me, right?"

I hoped that applied. He *was* supposed to look after my emotional wellbeing — asking him to protect me from drowning went a long way beyond that.

The shimmering hologram looked from me to the alien command console and back. Hesitantly reached out a paw. Paused. I held my breath, not wanting to risk distracting him.

With decisive motion, the hologram pressed the button. The forcefield holding me to the chair switched off instantly, dropping me into the ice-cold water with a scream.

My arm bashed into something hard under the surface and pain shot through me. Above me, the cracked glass creaked, and water poured into the cockpit. There wasn't much time. I picked myself up and splashed to Auric's side.

His seat was still above the rising waters, and the forcefield held him there. In the dim light of the instrument panel I couldn't see any obvious injuries. Biting my lip, I gave him a quick once over.

Still no movement from him, but his chest rose and fell slowly. Not dead, then. I breathed a sigh of relief, letting go of a tension I hadn't known I was holding in.

"Okay, good, you're alive," I said. "Now wake up! Or do you expect me to carry you out of here?"

No response. I shook him. Nothing. I hit his arm hard enough to make my hand sting.

No change.

The water rose around me, and the cracks in the window widened. Soon the glass would give and the water would crash in. Would I be able to swim to the surface after that? I didn't know. I couldn't even tell how deep we were.

"Please wake up," I said, pulling at Auric's arm. It was futile. Okay then, I'd have to handle this myself.

His chair still held him tight, but I could see the glow of the release button. I stretched over the alien as the water crept up my legs. This close, I could feel his heartbeat, his powerful pulse somehow reassuring even as I struggled to free him from his seat.

"Damn it, when I thought about being this close to you, I didn't expect you to be unconscious," I muttered, trying to distract myself from the growing feeling of doom as the ship sank. Good thing he couldn't hear me: I'd have rather gnawed my leg off than admit what I'd been thinking about him.

There! My fingers reached the button and I pushed. The forcefield vanished instantly and Auric's weight landed on me, sending the two of us crashing back into the icy water. For a moment I panicked, trapped under his weight, and then I squirmed free.

Now what? We were still trapped in the cockpit of the alien ship. There had to be emergency supplies somewhere — on a human ship there definitely would be, but I had no idea where to look. And I didn't have time to search, not with the water around my knees and rising fast.

"We're going to have to get out of here," I told Auric's unconscious form. Took a deep breath, then another. "You saved me, so I'm going to save you, but can you try not to weigh so damned much?"

I'd never thought that a man could have too much muscle, but then I'd never expected to have to carry one to safety. I'd just have to do my best. I took a deep breath and looked around for a way out.

Auric's belt still held the pistol he'd taken. I looked at it, bit my lip, and nodded. Not a great plan, but it would have to do. Fumbling the unfamiliar weight into my hand, I gripped it tight and tried to figure it out.

That looked like a safety, and that a trigger. Simple enough. I swallowed, hoping I had it figured out.

I hooked my arms under Auric's and aimed the gun upward. Took deep breaths, filling my lungs with the air we had left. And pulled the trigger.

Nothing happened. I flicked the safety the other way and tried again. Nothing. I frowned, looked at it again, gave it a smack. Still nothing. Either the controls were more complicated than they looked or it was out of charge. Either way, I wasn't going to get any use out of it.

With a creak, the glass bowed inward, cold water streaming down. The cockpit of a spaceship was built to keep air in, not water out, and as the ship sank deeper, the pressure outside grew.

"Fine. We'll just have to chance it." I don't know who I was speaking to, the unconscious alien or the hologram cat. Neither answered me.

I stood directly under the bowing glass, my arms linked around Auric's chest, holding tight and bracing myself. Breathing deeply, quickly, filling my lungs as much as possible, I waited for the inevitable.

Crack. The glass failed all at once, and the air around me rushed out in a bubble. I pushed off as hard as I could, letting it carry us out into the lake as the ship fell away into deep water.

Icy waters closed around us as I kicked for the surface, Auric's solid bulk pulling me down. Cursing silently, I struggled to keep my cool and swam as hard as I could. The cold sank into me, numbing me, and beneath us I saw the wrecked ship vanish, its few remaining lights blinking out.

My lungs burned and every muscle ached as I finally broke the surface, gasping for air. It tasted so sweet, so pure. It tasted like life. For a moment all I could do was lie back, holding Auric's head above the water and sucking in breath after breath.

Above me, fire streaked across the bright blue sky. It looked like a meteor shower, but I knew it for what it was — debris of the space battle raining down on the planet. Aliens and humans, scattered across the surface. How many lived and how many died? Pointless to guess, especially when it wasn't yet clear if *I'd* survived. I needed to make it to shore before my muscles gave out and we both drowned.

Lowering my gaze, I looked at the nearest land. Luckily for us, the lake we'd landed in wasn't that big, and the shore was close enough to swim to. On my own it wouldn't even have been hard. Dragging an unconscious alien warrior made it more of a task, and by the time I reached the rocky beach, I had no strength left.

The effort of pulling Auric up onto the stones nearly finished me, but I managed to get him above the tide line before I stopped.

My muscles burned with effort and I sat down beside him, hugging my knees and shivering. It took an effort to resist the urge to lie down and sleep, but if I did that I might never wake up. I needed help, or at least company. Something to give me focus.

I pressed Mr. Mews' on switch, and he shimmered into existence, proving that despite everything my wristband actually was waterproof. I smiled at the sight of the hologram scampering on the rocky beach as though he didn't have a care in the world.

"I can't believe how glad I am to see you," I told the hologram. He was the one thing in my life that hadn't been yanked away from me in the last hour, the only constant I had left.

Besides that, he had practical uses. He functioned as a communicator and a database, and he had his ultrasound to drive off predators. Okay, that was meant for use on Arcadia and I had no idea if it would work on this planet. And it would use up his batteries quickly if I tried to use it all the time.

"Can you contact anyone, Mr. Mews?" I wasn't surprised when he shook his head. The armband's radio only had a short range, intended for connecting to the *Wandering Star's* systems rather than contacting someone across a planet. "Worth a try. Tell me if you pick up any signals."

Mr. Mews nodded, then scampered off up the beach. I looked up at the nearby forest. Alien trees loomed, purplish leaves rustling in the wind, and I wondered what kind of wildlife was watching us. Had our crash-landing frightened off everything out there, or were predators deciding if we looked like lunch?

It didn't matter. I was in no state to fight off anything that came at us, so why worry about it? The only precaution I could take was telling Mr. Mews to turn on his ultrasound and hoping that worked.

Getting into shelter amongst the trees would be a lot better than resting beside the lake, exposed to the elements. But there was no way that I was going to drag the alien warrior any further. Frankly I was surprised I'd managed to move him this far, and it had used up all my reserves.

I need to rest, I thought. *Just for a little bit.* But if I stopped now, I'd freeze. My clothes were waterlogged with the lake's icy water and my teeth chattered from the cold.

There was nothing for it. We'd have to huddle for warmth. The thought caused a strange fluttering in my stomach as I pulled off the outer layers of my uniform and wrung the water from them. The sun would dry them while I rested.

I looked down at the unconscious alien warrior who'd saved me but whose people had caused all this pain. It was impossible to decide what I felt about him, but we needed each other's warmth if we were going to survive.

At least, that's what I told myself as I lay down against him.

For warmth, that's all, I told myself. But I couldn't deny that the press of Auric's muscular body felt good in other ways too. Perhaps it was the near brush with death, but my body responded to him and a blush spread across me as I snuggled close.

Darkness closed about me almost instantly, and my

last thought was a half-dream moment in which I felt Auric holding me. I smiled happily at that, and slipped away into a dreamless slumber.

～

WHEN I WOKE, I felt warm and comfortable. For a moment I wondered if it had all been a dream and I was still aboard the *Wandering Star*, but no. My cabin didn't have a cool breeze blowing through it, the bed might be uncomfortable, but it didn't feel like lying on rocks, and there shouldn't be the sound of waves.

Crap. That wasn't a dream. I'm stranded on an alien planet with...

My thoughts trailed off as I remembered Auric, the feel of his body against mine.

I forced my eyes open and sat up in a shower of leaves. Auric had left but he'd left me covered up in a surprisingly snug nest. I flushed bright red at the thought of him waking to find me clinging to him, only wearing my underwear.

The thought sent a tingle running through me, a mix of shame and excitement. I pushed those thoughts aside and scrambled to my feet, looking around.

Now that I'd rested I could appreciate my surroundings more. The sun stood high in the sky and the lake glittered, beautiful and strange. While the trees above me were like nothing I'd seen before, they were at least recognizably *trees*. Their leaves were an odd shade of purple and the trunks grew in strange shapes, like clawed hands grasping for the sky.

Life existed here. Hopefully that meant that we would be able to survive.

Don't get ahead of yourself, I thought. *There might not be anything to eat here, or the water might be poisonous, or anything.* There was a reason life in the Exploration Service was a way to fame and fortune — the adventurers looking for potential colony worlds faced a lot of danger.

We colonists only settled on safe worlds, ones that had been explored and checked. Arcadia, for example. Not wherever we'd crashed.

I looked around for any sign of life. Nothing. Had the crash scared off all the local wildlife, or was there none to frighten away? Or was something I couldn't see or hear creeping up on me? I shivered despite the warmth of the sunlight, wrapping my arms around myself and wishing I had some kind of weapon.

"Food," Auric said, his rough voice making me jump and squeak. I spun to see him emerging from the forest with a small animal in hand. Dark fur, matted with blood, and sharp teeth. I stared at the dead animal, trying to see it as food.

My rumbling stomach helped.

"Don't sneak up on me like that," I said, then tried to figure out how to repeat it in Galtrade. Too many words I didn't know.

Auric seemed to get the gist, though, or at least the gesture he made looked apologetic. But his eyes didn't apologize as he stared at me, and I remembered how much skin I was showing.

Blushing bright red, I looked around for my clothes. They hung where I'd left them, drying on a rock near the water. With as much dignity as I could muster, I walked over to retrieve them.

Auric's eyes never left me, and the lust in his gaze was as unnerving as it was exciting. There was no artifice in his look, no dishonesty: he liked looking at me and didn't pretend otherwise. And I couldn't deny that I liked being looked at.

This wasn't like the guys back on Earth or McKenzie aboard the *Wandering Star*. It was more honest, and more straightforward. Somehow I felt that I could trust Auric. Maybe because I liked looking at him just as much.

It's not like I didn't take a good look earlier, I reminded myself as I pulled the uniform on. It was dry, thank god, and when I turned back to face him, Auric smiled and said something I couldn't follow.

I really need to work on my Galtrade. Language lessons could wait, though. For now, I was starving and we needed to cook the ... whatever Auric had caught.

He sat beside the lake, a small pile of firewood next to him and a perplexed expression on his face as he tried to light it. I almost laughed as he rubbed two sticks together — his technique was *awful*. It looked like he had heard that it was possible but never tried.

"Let me try," I told him. It had been a long time since I'd tried to start a fire without tools, but my father had taught me how. At least I had something to contribute to this meal.

It took longer than I'd hoped. Rubbing two sticks together is a terrible way to start a fire, but eventually I coaxed a small flame out and, adding dry leaves carefully, grew it into a bigger one. Meanwhile, Auric set to cleaning his kill. By the time the fire was going, he had the animal ready to cook on a wooden spit.

For a moment I worried about poison. Would we even be able to eat this? But worrying about that wouldn't help. We had nothing else to eat, and no way to test for poisons. If the animals weren't edible, we'd starve.

Plus, the thing smelled delicious. Whatever his other talents, Auric knew how to cook in the wild. I struggled to wait for the meat to be done, my mouth watering.

Eventually he was satisfied, pulling the cooked meat off the stick and onto some large leaves. It tasted as good as it smelled, though that might be my hunger speaking.

We ate in silence, and while there wasn't much meat on the animal, it was enough to stop my stomach complaining for the time being.

"What now?" I asked as I wiped my hands clean with some leaves. "Where to?"

Auric started to say something, then frowned. "Where is ship?"

I pointed to the water and he nodded grimly. He must have guessed as much — where else could it have gone? — but the confirmation hit him hard. No wonder. Without that ship and the equipment inside it we were on our own with only our wits to protect us.

There was one bright side. If I had to be stranded on an unknown planet with someone I barely knew, at least it was Auric.

12

AURIC

I looked out at the placid lake and tried to control my urge to swear. If I started, I wouldn't stop. All our supplies, all our gear, everything that would make survival on this planet possible, all of it was down there on the lake floor.

I'm not, I reminded myself. *And neither is Tamara. As long as we're alive, everything else is secondary.*

That might not be for long, though. The woods were too quiet, and the animal I'd caught had been the only life I'd seen. Perhaps the noise of the crash had scared everything else away? I hoped so — that would mean that we'd find more game to hunt as we traveled.

But we couldn't stay here.

"We must move," I told Tamara. It took a couple of tries to get the meaning across, but when she understood she nodded. Good.

She didn't look like much of a survivor, but she'd already proved me wrong once. Without her, I'd be on the bottom of the lake along with the ship. It warmed my heart to know she had the determination to drag me up onto the beach, even if I wished she'd brought the survival pack with her. But how would she even have known where to look for it?

Tamara gestured around us and shrugged. I nodded: which direction to go in was the first question we had to answer. I tried to remember the terrain from before the crash, but those memories were hazy and I'd only had a moment to look around.

If I don't know, then one direction is as good as another. Better to get moving and figure it out later. And better for Tamara if she thinks I know where we're going.

I didn't want her to worry, and that meant looking as confident as I could. *Perhaps I've failed every other human, but I can shield her from harm and worry. That's something.*

"There," I told her, pointing uphill through the trees with as much confidence as I could muster. With luck we'd be able to see something from the high ground, and if not, at least we were moving.

She nodded, and I caught a little grin. Perhaps she wasn't fooled, but as long as she was amused rather than frightened I didn't mind.

There was nothing to pack up at our little camp, so I made sure our fire was out and then turned my back and walked into the trees. Tamara followed, hanging back a little to start with but catching up as the shadows settled around us.

The forest wasn't thick, but the tree canopy blocked

enough light to make me wary. There was something ominous about the silence that surrounded us and I felt on edge. Still, it was better than being out in the open. I'd lived too long on a spaceship to be comfortable with the sky above me.

I kept myself alert for any predators that might be in the area, hoping there was nothing large enough to see us as prey. Whatever animals hunted here wouldn't have any fear of us, and I didn't want to take any chances.

After a little while, Tamara spoke up behind me.

"I must learn more words?"

I looked around, frowning, and she pointed at a tree. Made a noise. *Oh. She wants to learn more Galtrade?*

If we could communicate, we'd be better able to survive. At least that's what I told myself as I started to trade words with her. In truth it was more than that. Speaking meant I felt less alone, and hearing her voice warmed my soul.

It was bad enough being stranded on this planet, but being here on my own would have driven me insane. Marooning people on isolated planets was a punishment for the worst traitors of the Silver Band.

It was the kind of fate that Zaren deserved, and the punishment he'd have decreed for me if he had the chance. Growling, I tried not to dwell on that and concentrated on the language lessons.

Fortunately, Tamara had a basic grasp of the language and she was a quick study. Galtrade was an ugly, awkward tongue, designed for ease of use rather than poetry. But it was a lot better than nothing, and with the help of her virtual cat the human learned quickly.

The hologram made me smile and shake my head. Simulating a small mammal was a curious use of computing power, but it came in handy as a translator and there was something appealing about the little creature.

I wondered how the hologram still functioned when my technology didn't. Perhaps the humans' batteries were simply too primitive to be targeted by the taveshi? I hoped so — that would mean that the *Wandering Star* might be salvageable. It was a distant hope, but something to cling to.

It took most of the day for us to get to the top of the hill I'd started us on, and the sun touched the horizon as we clambered to the top. On the far side was a steep drop, and from the edge we stared out over a deep forest.

"Oh good," Tamara said, followed by an unfamiliar word in her own language. I recognized a swear word when I heard one. "More trees."

"Could be worse," I pointed out. "Could be a desert."

That wasn't a word she knew and she had to ask the cat for help. After a quick back-and-forth she nodded reluctantly. Forest might not be the easiest terrain to move through, but it was a lot better than some of the options.

We both fell silent, looking out over the purple-red

trees and hoping for some hint of where we should go next.

"There," Tamara said, grabbing my arm and pointing out over the canopy. "Look. Smoke!"

I followed her outstretched arm, trying to resist the distraction of her touch. As close as we'd been all day, the feel of her fingers on my skin was still enough to make my heart beat faster and it wasn't easy to keep my attention on where she was pointing.

It took me a moment to see it. The thin plume of smoke rising from the forest was hard to spot but unmistakable once she pointed it out. I squinted, trying to see more detail. A native camp? Another crash site?

The forest looked disturbed, but from this distance I couldn't be sure. Probably another crashed Silver Band raider, then, or a colony pod from the *Wandering Star*. I didn't want to rule out the possibility of sapient natives, though, or even other space travelers.

It didn't matter: it gave us a direction to go, and that was what we needed. Whoever or whatever waited for us, it would be better than striking out with no goal in mind.

"Too far for today," I said, reluctantly estimating the distance. There was no way we'd make it before nightfall and navigating in the dark would be impossible. That smoke plume was hard enough to see now. "We must camp."

For a moment I thought Tamara would mutiny at that. She looked exhausted, but her eyes sparkled as she stared out at the distant smoke. Her body was practically vibrating with hope.

"Tamara," I said, voice firm. "We will not reach them today. If we try, we will just get lost in the woods. Make a fire."

My tone of command made her turn back to me, her jaw clamping shut and face darkening. I met her gaze levelly, not giving an inch, and after a long moment she nodded. Reluctance written in every inch of her body, she looked around for fallen wood.

I nodded, relieved. If she'd tried to run off, I'd have had to restrain her, and then where would we be? I could hardly keep her tied up for the rest of the journey, however long that took.

But if I let her run off on her own, she'd be dead in a day. That was intolerable, and if I had to keep her prisoner to save her life, I would.

Where did that thought come from? I asked myself, tearing my eyes away from the human female. Her safety meant more to me than my own, and I couldn't think straight when I thought that she was in danger.

If this was the vaunted mating instinct of my people, then I wasn't sure I wanted anything to do with it.

∽

LEAVING Tamara to make the fire, I took to the woods to hunt. My mood darkened as I moved away from her and I thought about our situation. While I was with the human I kept my mood light to encourage her.

Now, in the darkness of the forest, I could feel the rage and pain in my soul. I refused to let it distract me from my task. We needed something to eat, and there was no safe way to test the local plants for poison. The animals were more likely to be safe to eat, and the forest was slowly returning to life around us. On the one hand that meant that hunting was easier than it had been, but on the other I worried that there might be predators loose in the woods now.

I didn't dare stray far from Tamara, which limited my hunt. But some of the local animals were easy prey, and it wasn't too long before I had caught four small mammal-like creatures. Enough for a meal.

Returning to the cliff where we'd camped, I saw Tamara waiting for me beside a small fire. She'd been careful to keep it away from the trees, which was good — we had no need to risk a forest fire.

I hoped that the other fire wouldn't spread. The last thing we needed was to walk into an inferno, but there was nothing we could do about it. At least the trees didn't seem dry enough to catch all that easily, but what did I know of that? I'd hunted on planets often enough — I'd never lived on one.

Tamara looked up as I stepped into the circle of firelight, her eyes shining. The ruddy glow of the flames flicked over her and despite my mood I couldn't help smiling at the sight of her.

Muddy, exhausted, scratched by the undergrowth

we'd pushed our way through — still she looked beautiful, desirable, wonderful. A low, hungry growl escaped my throat before I got control of myself.

Do not presume, I told myself. *She is not yours to take. That's exactly the crime that you broke with the Silver Band over.*

Tamara deserved to make her own choices, and right now she had none. But I couldn't help thinking back to how good it had felt to wake that morning, with her pressed against me in the bed of leaves.

With an effort, I turned my back on her and sat down to clean my kills. She deserved better than me anyway. I was a traitor to my Band, and even in that I'd failed.

I would make sure she got to her people safe and sound, if I could. And then she'd be free of me. Hopefully the *Wandering Star* or some of its colony pods had made it down to the planet safely and in walking distance.

If not, I'd have to find a Silver Band ship and work out how to get its hyperdrive working again. Once I'd defeated whatever the taveshi used to discharge our batteries, I would take Tamara to a human world. I twitched at the thought of that journey, weeks or months of traveling with her at my side. The temptation would be unbearable.

Don't think about that now. We need to survive the night and the next few days. Then I can worry about what comes next.

When I turned back to the fire she waited,

watching me. I tried to smile at her, to look reassuringly confident, but I saw from her eyes that it didn't work.

We cooked the mammals in silence, the soft crackle of the fire filling our small camp. They tasted good, delicious even, and it was a joy to share such a meal with the human.

Afterward we looked out over the forest in silence. The stars had come out, constellations alien to both of us filling the sky, and two moons rose over the horizon. One large, slow, half-full. The other small and fast, crossing the sky quickly.

Tamara moved closer, sitting against me, and I felt her shiver. Instinctively I put my arm around her, pulling her in to shelter her from the cold.

For a moment she tensed and then she relaxed against me, an arm going around my waist and holding tight. Now it was my turn to tense. Her warm body against mine was enough to drive my instincts crazy, and she filled my senses. She smelled so good, like flowers I couldn't name, and I wanted more than anything to grab her and take her.

But I would not give in to that temptation. Tamara belonged with her own kind, and I refused to take advantage of her. No matter how much my body craved the touch of her skin.

"Will we live?" she asked quietly, resting her head against my shoulder, oblivious to the fight going on inside me.

"Yes." I let none of my doubts show in my voice.

"You will return home safe, I swear by the Eternal Flame."

How much that oath was worth I couldn't say. It was a sacred oath of my people, but it was also the one I'd broken when I turned against the Silver Band. Still, I intended to keep this one and to make sure that she went back to her people unharmed.

Tamara muttered something under her breath in that strange language I knew nothing of. Sad and lonely. I could sympathize. We were both alone here, each potentially the last of our people alive on this planet.

I squeezed her shoulder, intending to comfort her. She let out a hushed breath and turned to me, her breath warm on my skin…

Standing abruptly, I stepped away from her. No more. I couldn't face it. If I spent another second touching her, my self-control might snap.

13

TAMARA

Auric turned his back and stalked out into the darkness of the forest, leaving me staring after him. My insides knotted from pain and confusion as I watched him go. What had I done to annoy him?

The tension in his shoulders as he vanished into the shadows made me want to throw something at him. I'd thought, just for a second, that we were having a moment. But no, now he was storming off again, cold and distant.

Why do I have such bad taste in men? I'd asked myself that question a million times over the years, but today it bit deep. Leaving Earth, I'd hoped that my string of bad luck would end.

Now here I was, stuck in the middle of nowhere with the sexiest man I'd ever met, and he stormed off rather than holding me. Fucking great.

"It's probably for the best," I told myself out loud, pushing a few more sticks into the fire and watching sparks fly. "Do I even want him? He's a space pirate. And a dick."

But my body didn't agree. And he *had* saved my life. Along with anyone else who'd survived the attack on the *Wandering Star* — I tried not to think about the possibility that the crash had killed them all.

"What do you think, Mr. Mews?" I asked my wristband, and the holographic cat appeared. He wore a quizzical expression and had no answer for me.

Still, somehow it cheered me up to see the little fake kitten. He purred and mimed a headbutt at my hand. It was enough to make me smile. Maybe whoever had decided to give us these damned virtual pets had been onto something?

"You're right," I told the cat. "No point in worrying about it."

"Mrr," the cat agreed. I sat back and watched the stars going past. Was one of them Earth's sun? I had no idea. Maybe McKenzie would know, if he was still alive. It was strange to think of him stranded somewhere on this planet.

"I guess it could be worse, I could be trapped with him instead." God, that would have been awful. I could just imagine him leering at me, almost hear him make a comment about 'repopulating the planet.' I shuddered at the thought. Being stuck with Auric was a lot better by comparison.

Frustrating as he was, I'd rather be with him than any human I knew. I wondered what that said about me as I drifted off to sleep.

MR. MEWS WOKE ME, the pathetic little noise he made cutting into my dreams and pulling me back to consciousness. One of the useful tricks of a companion hologram — his ultrasonic alarm was impossible to sleep through.

A half-remembered dream faded as my eyes opened reluctantly. I couldn't remember much, only something about a blue-skinned giant pinning me to the bed of leaves, his muscular body pressed to mine.

I wasn't happy with Mr. Mews for dragging me out of that dream. Only half awake, I glared at the hologram wondering why he'd woken me. The sky was still dark, unfamiliar constellations shining down on me.

"What is it?" I hissed, instinctively quiet. I was alone in the camp, and the fire had burned low while I slept. Where was Auric?

The holographic cat looked out into the darkness and hissed a warning. For a moment I was tempted to pull off the wristband and throw it over the side of the cliff, but something stopped me. Was Mr. Mews really trying to warn me about something?

A faint sound in the darkness made the hairs on the back of my neck stand up on end. Just the wind? Or an alien predator prowling closer? I wondered if I smelled like a tasty treat to anything that lived here.

We can eat the animals here, I thought, heart hammering. *That means that the local wildlife can eat us, right?*

That was *not* a pleasant notion, and I wished that

Auric was back with me. Without him I was defenseless against whatever was out there hunting me.

Almost defenseless, anyway. I'd left Mr. Mews' ultrasound off to save his batteries, but now I wondered if that had been a good idea. No point in saving it and being eaten.

Only this isn't Arcadia, I reminded myself. Would the same thing that stopped a predator on Arcadia work on this planet? That seemed a dangerous thing to pin my hopes on. What if it made things worse?

I looked at the hologram, the tiny translucent cat staring into the darkness. Under the shadow of the trees something big moved towards the camp. I grabbed a fallen branch and lifted it like a club. Not much of a weapon, but the best I could find in a hurry.

The shadow in the forest moved closer, silent and deadly. The size of a tiger or bigger. I suppressed a whimper — how was I supposed to fight a *tiger?*

Should I shout, try to scare it off? Or would that just attract attention? Maybe I should call for Auric, but I had no idea how far away he was. If that drew an attack before he reached me it wouldn't do any good. Was he even close enough to hear?

The makeshift club was slippery in my hand as I raised it high and whispered to Mr. Mews. "Predator defenses on, please."

The hologram arched his back, hissing a sound that spiraled up out of the range of human hearing. It made me wince for a second and then I couldn't hear it anymore.

Whatever was out there could, though. But instead of fleeing in fear as it was supposed to, it roared a challenge and pounced out of the cover of the forest. I stood frozen to the spot, staring at the monster.

It was huge, catlike, and ferocious. Like a tiger if tigers had a cluster of writhing tentacles around their mouths. Eyes gleamed red in the firelight and the tentacles tasted the air as it stalked forward with deadly grace.

I hefted my club as threateningly as I could. Drew myself up to my full height — somewhere I'd read that was a good idea to look big. But the alien tiger-thing looked too enraged to care, roaring and pacing towards me. The tentacles around its mouth spread wide, lashing the air, and I backed off quickly. I hoped putting the remains of the fire between me and the monster would keep it away from me.

It ignored the flames, bounding towards me faster than I could back away. Far from driving the beast off, Mr. Mews' ultrasound was sending the creature wild with rage. Its eyes were fixed on my wristband, and it let out an angry growl. The sound made me want to drop the club and run, but I knew turning my back would mean my death.

God damned lowest-bidder contracts, I thought. *The ultrasound's meant to scare predators not piss them off.* "Mr. Mews, ultrasound off!"

A feeling of pressure left the air, but the tentacle-mouthed tiger didn't forget about me when the sounds stopped. It darted forward, mighty paw swiping at me, and I jumped back around the remains of the fire. A wild swing with the club achieved nothing, not even connecting with the creature.

Behind it I heard other roars and howls. The whole forest was alive with movement now. *Is that all down to Mr. Mews? Did that sound piss off every animal on the damned planet?*

I didn't have time to worry about that. The tentacle tiger leaped for me with a deafening roar and my heel hit a rock as I tried to dodge, sending me tumbling backward. That saved my life — the creature's claws slashed through the space where my face would have been if I hadn't fallen.

In desperation, I screamed and swung the club again. This time I connected with a satisfying *thunk*. The impact vibrated up my arm, nearly shaking the branch out of my hand, and the creature reared back and yowled in pain.

For a moment I dared to hope it would turn tail and run. Instead it lunged in, striking fast as lightning. I swung at its face again, but it was ready for me and tentacles wrapped around my hand. A sharp, stinging pain flashed through me followed by numbness as I lost all feeling in my right arm.

Crap. My hand spasmed, the club falling from my numb fingers, and I tried to scramble away from the creature. No chance: it was too fast, on me before I'd gone a step, and I barely managed to avoid a swipe of its claws by tumbling to the ground.

I tried to rise, but it was already there, venomous

tentacles writhing above me as it lowered its awful face to feed. I pulled up my arms, knowing it was futile. But I wasn't going to wait for my death without trying to fend it off.

The hologram of Mr. Mews reared up in front of it, roaring with a volume and ferocity I'd never heard before. The creature looked startled, staring at the tiny floating cat, and then grabbed with its tentacles.

Which passed through Mr. Mews, unable to grip a hologram. The tentacled tiger made a confused noise that would have been adorable if it wasn't about to kill and eat me. Trying again, it swiped through Mr. Mews, who reared up again, small paws batting at the tentacles as though this was a game.

Anything that kept the creature at bay was fine by me. But what could I do to take advantage of the distraction? My right hand was useless, and even if I'd been able to grab a rock, I didn't think I'd be able to do anything with it. Not against this monster.

All I'd do is get its attention back on me, and that was the last thing I wanted.

Taking a deep breath, I tried to get my feet braced and ready to kick. At least with my boots on the stingers in those tentacles might not be able to get me. It wasn't much to pin my hopes on, but it was all I had.

The creature tired of its attempts to fight Mr. Mews and focused past him at me. Hissing, it raised a paw, and I knew it was now or never.

I kicked it in the mouth with all my strength. It howled, tumbling away, shocked that I'd dared to fight back again. I felt the lash of the tentacles against my boot, but nothing got through and as soon as it was away from me I rolled to my feet.

It was already bounding towards me. My foolish, vain thought that I could escape it was all for nothing, and I braced myself for death. The beast closed on me in slow motion, tentacles splayed wide and mouth aimed at my face.

At the last second, something hit it from the side. The impact knocked it off course and it flew past me, hitting the ground, rolling over and over.

Auric clung to its side, grimly hanging on as the two of them tumbled across the camp. The creature's claws tore at him, but he paid it no heed. His own claws dug in deep, and the monster roared in pain, tentacles flailing.

My heart leaped into my mouth and I stood paralyzed, watching him come to my rescue again. The creature was bigger than he was, and perhaps more dangerous, but he hadn't hesitated to put his life on the line for me.

So why are you hesitating? A voice inside my head asked. *He needs your help too.*

It was true. The creature's claws had opened deep gashes in Auric's side, and while the monster was bleeding it didn't seem to be slowing. The two seemed evenly matched and while I was confident that Auric would win, I didn't want to think about what condition he'd be in afterward.

Mr. Mews looked at me from my wrist, extending

one virtual paw towards the fire. I tried to shake myself out of my shock and staggered over to the flames. Maybe the hologram had a good idea, and I couldn't think of anything else to try.

One piece of wood was large enough that the end of it wasn't on fire. Grabbing it with my good hand, I pulled it from the flames and lunged toward the fight in a desperate swing.

The flames blinded me and my swing went over both of their heads, but the monster snarled and backed away. Yep, it didn't like the fire. Okay. I could do this.

My next swing connected with the creature's flank, and it howled in outrage. A deadly claw-swipe missed me by inches as Auric dragged the creature back. It turned on him, snarling and snapping at his arm, and I hammered the burning brand down on its paw.

At last it seemed to have enough, turning and bounding away into the shadows. With its dark coloration it vanished into the night instantly, leaving us panting, bleeding and sore.

A laugh escaped my lips. Weirdly, I'd never felt so alive.

"Not funny," Auric said, panting for breath and picking himself up. The claw wounds on his arms and chest looked painful but not deadly, and the serious expression he wore couldn't quite hide the exhilaration in his eyes.

We'd survived another deadly threat together. I laughed louder, tossing the brand back into the fire and sitting down hard. My hand throbbed painfully, whatever venom the creature's tentacles carried eating away at me. I didn't care: we were alive and nothing else mattered.

"You could have died," Auric rumbled, ignoring his own wounds to look at mine. "Let me handle fighting."

I looked at him, unable to keep a straight face. "Seriously? You nearly got yourself killed protecting me, and you think I'd just let you die?"

Half of that was in Galtrade, the other half in English, but the message got across. Auric's mouth twitched as he tried look stern and didn't quite manage. Slowly enough that I could follow, he told me: "If I die protecting you, that is my choice. I won't see you hurt."

Overprotective he might be, but that wasn't an idle boast. I'd just seen that he was willing to put his life between me and harm, and it wasn't easy to argue with him after that.

I did my best. "And it's my choice if I want to risk my life for you. If you'd lost that fight, it would have killed me next."

Auric shook his head, growling and unconvinced. Had he even understood what I'd tried to say? But at least he didn't argue. Instead, he grabbed my throbbing right arm and looked at the wounds.

The tentacles had left dark welts around my forearm, and I could barely feel his touch. But when he squeezed, the pain made me cry out.

"Sorry," he said, and I shook my head.

"You're trying to help," I replied. He was silent, looking at my arm in the firelight.

"No," he said after a moment, quiet and hard. His anger wasn't at me, or even the tiger-thing. It had turned inward, at himself. "I should have been here. You could have died."

He looked up, his eyes full of pain. I could barely stand to meet his gaze.

"But I didn't," I tried. "You saved me."

"Too little," he said, his emotions vanishing behind a wall of ice again. "Too late. Just like always."

14

AURIC

The good news was that the beast's venom wasn't deadly. Its stinging tentacles were paralytic rather than fatal, and I wondered what had caused such a powerful predator to evolve stings like that. Either they hunted something that needed the poison to bring it down, or it was a defense against something higher up the food chain.

If something hunted those creatures, it would be an interesting challenge, but not one I wanted to meet with Tamara in tow. She'd suffered enough from my failure to protect her as it was.

Luckily, there didn't seem to be any permanent damage. Her fingers started to work again quickly, and by the time the sun rose she had control over her whole arm. Though she tried to hide it from me, Tamara was still in pain — but she would recover.

I hadn't failed her too badly, thank the blessed ones. Tamara would return to her people in one piece, though the marks the stingers had left around her wrist remained. A reminder of my failure.

The hologram cat watched as I examined her, big eyes full of curiosity. Once I'd finished examining Tamara, I turned to him.

"Thank you," I said gravely. "You served your mistress well, better than I did."

It might be a computer simulation of a cat, but it deserved the acknowledgement. Without this Mr. Mews, Tamara might have died before I reached her.

The cat meowed back at me. I doubted it understood a word I'd said, but that didn't matter. Reaching out carefully, I brushed its little head, feeling the forcefield push back at me gently. The little purring noise it gave off made me feel a bit better, and I managed to smile.

Tamara was smiling too, watching with amused patience as I spoke with her hologram. I pulled my hand back and took a deep breath. Time to focus on practical matters — we had a long way to go today, and hadn't gotten much rest.

Before we set out, I found a couple of long straight branches and broke them off. Without tools it wasn't easy to shape the ends into points, but I did my best with my claws. Holding the tips into our small fire hardened them.

Crude spears were better than going unarmed.

Tamara tried to speak to me a few more times, but what was there to say? She might not blame me for this mess but I knew better. The sooner I got her back to her own kind the better — then she'd be safe and I'd be beyond the temptation I felt.

She might be my mate, my khara, the female fate intended for me. That didn't make me worthy of her, and I would not let myself fall into the trap of thinking I was.

Setting out towards the source of the smoke we'd seen the day before, I kept a careful eye on the foliage around us. Now that we knew there were predators who would attack us we had to be doubly careful, and I would take no chances with Tamara's safety.

While my attention was on the forest, Tamara turned hers to her wristband, speaking in hushed tones to Mr. Mews. The third time she caught me glancing at her, she shrugged and tried to explain.

"You can make these," she said lifting the spear I'd given her. "I am an engineer. Perhaps I can fix the sound."

I hid my doubts. Perhaps she'd be able to adjust the ultrasound to make it useful, perhaps not, but it seemed unlikely she would make things *worse.* At least it gave her something to concentrate on doing, which was valuable on its own.

Without a subject to test her changes on, it was a moot point. Nothing emerged from the undergrowth to threaten us and we continued through the eerie quiet of the forest. Most of the morning passed in silence as we marched through the woods until we reached a small stream. I stepped over it, only to hear Tamara stop at the bank and sit down.

"Come. We cannot wait," I said, looking back at her. She looked up at me, rebellious, and didn't move.

"I need to drink, Auric," she said slowly, as though to a child. "Maybe you can go days without water, but a human can't."

I growled at that but relented. If her species needed more water than a prytheen warrior, then I couldn't argue with biology. I simply had to hope that the water was safe to drink, and any microbes that lived there wouldn't bother a human.

Tamara cupped her hands in the swift-running water and brought it up to her mouth, sipping and sighing happily. If she knew the risks of drinking unpurified water, she didn't let them bother her. I couldn't help smiling. Despite all the danger that she'd been through, despite the brushes with death, she still found joy in this simple pleasure. And her joy lit up my heart.

Instinct took me a step closer before I could control myself, and I sank into a crouch opposite her. There was no sign of danger, and her happy smile was infectious. The planet might be dangerous, but that didn't mean we couldn't take these moments of calm joy for ourselves. Rather, it was a reason to savor what pleasures we found — each one might be our last.

Tamara drank her fill and then turned that beautiful smile on me. The sight made me feel alive, and I couldn't help returning her expression.

"See, I knew you could be happy," she said with a laugh. I grimaced, but she had a point. For a second I'd forgotten my pain in the simple pleasure of her company. Stranded on a planet that had tried to kill her, Tamara still found cheer and courage. I could do no less.

Perhaps being stranded here wouldn't be too bad?

~

THE CLOSER WE came to our destination, the easier the trail became to follow. Where the ship had entered the forest, trees lay uprooted and scattered along the path of the crash. Unlike us, this pilot hadn't been able to find a safe place to land. Parts of the ship lay scattered amongst the trees, damaged enough that I couldn't tell if we were following a Silver Band raider or one of the human colony pods.

There goes any hope of flying out of here, I thought as I looked at damage. Glancing at Tamara, I saw her face fall as she reached the same conclusion. Injured from the fight, the walk hadn't been kind to her. She leaned on her spear as we travelled, and both of us had been hoping to find a useable vehicle at our journey's end.

Now it looked like the best we could hope for was a wreck worth scavenging.

"On the bright side," she said, forcing cheer into her voice, "at least this way we know there'll be something to find at the end of this mess."

I nodded, acknowledging her point. If the ship had landed intact, it might well have left before we got to it.

We followed the trail of destruction, and I tried to

stay alert. If there were any prytheen survivors waiting for us, they wouldn't be friendly to us. Humans, on the other hand, would only be hostile to *me*. That was definitely better, but I didn't intend to get myself shot.

I needn't have worried. The path of wrecked trees ended with a Silver Band heavy raider, lying crashed and crumpled in a crater on the forest floor. The impact had shattered the trees around it to splinters, and we were lucky that the fires the crash had started hadn't spread.

Scavenging birds erupted skyward as we left the trees and approached the wreck. That wasn't a good sign, and neither was the smell. The stench of death and decay had settled over the crash site.

"Stay here," I told Tamara. She looked rebellious, but this was no time for her to push me. I gave her a hard stare and after a long moment she relented.

"Fine. I'll keep watch."

If Tamara wanted to use that as the reason to stay out of the ship, I'd take it. As long as she didn't follow me inside to face what was sure to be a scene of horrors — she'd seen enough for a lifetime already, and I would spare her any further harm.

The ship lay tilted at an angle, the windows cracked and broken, and the hatch didn't respond to my command as I approached. I had to pry the damaged armorglass out of the cockpit window with my spear to climb inside.

Into a charnel house. The remains of the raider's crew were scattered across the cockpit in a gory mess where their personal forcefields had failed on impact. I glanced back over my shoulder to make sure that Tamara wasn't following — she'd turned out to be tougher than I'd expected but I doubted that she had the constitution for a sight like this.

I made my search quick. A quick check of the ship itself confirmed my fears: the battery pods were dead. The taveshi weapon had drained them completely, leaving this ship with only emergency power. And that had been used up in the crash, trying to keep the pilots alive.

But some emergency supplies survived, tucked away in a pack under the console. I hauled them to the broken window and threw the bag outside. Anything that had gotten through the crash intact wouldn't be broken by the drop to the forest floor.

There were two blaster pistols too. That gave me a moment of hope as I wiped the displays clean. If they still functioned Tamara and I would be in a much better position.

No. The displays were as dead as the ship's systems, the batteries drained completely. Whatever weapon the taveshi had used to disable the Silver Band's ships hadn't stopped there. That was a frightening level of technology, and more than that: it meant that we were stuck on this planet.

I reminded myself that Tamara's hologram still worked. Hopefully that meant that the humans' spaceship would still function too. If there was any hope for us to escape this world it would be the *Wandering Star*.

I put that thought out of my mind and discarded the useless pistols. No point in carrying useless weight, not when we had so far to travel.

On the verge of leaving I looked back at the bodies and frowned, wondering if I'd known these warriors. Their corpses were in a bad enough state that I couldn't tell, and guilt ate at me.

Whoever they were, these warriors had been part of my family until a few cycles ago. Now, they lay dead because of my actions. If I hadn't warned the humans, if I hadn't helped them, they would still be alive.

Don't fall into that trap. My father's remembered voice was clear and I could almost feel his hand on my shoulder. *They chose their path, not you. They thought the humans were defenseless and attacked them — what came of that dishonorable action is on their heads, not yours.*

That sounded like what he would say, but that didn't help me fight off my guilt. But there was nothing to do now. My course was set and turning back would only make things worse. All I could offer the dead were prayers.

"Find peace in the next life, warriors of the Band," I said formally. Whether I still had the authority to conduct the funerary rites I didn't know, but they couldn't *hurt.* "Go to meet the ancestors and tell them you fell in honorable battle."

Perhaps it was my imagination, but the cockpit felt a little less oppressive after I'd said the words. Perhaps their spirits had gone on to rest, perhaps it was all in my mind.

"Auric!" Tamara's shout pulled my attention out of the fallen ship, and without hesitating I dropped out of the broken window. She had her spear leveled at the forest, and I heard movement out there amongst the trees. Something big. Bigger than the beast that had hunted us last night, perhaps. Either that, or more than one animal approached. Neither option was good.

I grabbed up my spear and stepped between her and the danger. Probably it would be a carrion eater drawn by the smell of death, but it might still see us as potential meals.

"We should move," I said quietly. "The bodies attract scavengers."

Not words I'd taught her. She looked confused, then down at her wrist. Her pet hologram hissed a translation at her and she paled slightly but nodded. Together we grabbed the supplies I'd found and retreated from the clearing, leaving the ship to whatever animals were prowling the forest.

A low and threatening growl followed us. That was a good sign — a hunting animal would usually be silent. A predator making noise was sending a warning, wanting us to know we were on its territory. Hopefully that meant it just wanted us to leave.

But the sound was echoed by another ahead of us, and then a third to our left.

"We're surrounded," Tamara said, her voice trembling and quiet. She turned to point her spear towards the underbrush behind us. Edging to the right, away from whatever was in the forest.

I put a hand on her shoulder, gripping gently but firmly and holding her back. She flinched, paused, looked around at me.

"I know this trick," I told her, hoping she'd understand. "They are herding us."

Tamara's eyes widened, and she whipped the spear around to point at the gap she'd been heading to. An invitingly empty-seeming bit of forest which I knew better than to enter. I'd played that trick often, luring the enemy into an ambush with my clan.

The thought of them brought a pang to my heart. I was their alpha and they needed me, but I had left them behind to protect the humans. They would understand, of course — they were honorable warriors, protectors of the Code. I wondered how many had followed to help me, how many were stranded somewhere else on this planet.

I wished they were with me now. Even a handful of prytheen warriors at my side would make this easy. But instead I had to defend my khara from danger alone, and there was only one way I knew to defeat this trap.

Picking the direction of the loudest growl, I lunged. Leaping into the undergrowth, spear darting out, I aimed by sound rather than sight. The growl cut off in a sharp yelp of shock and pain, and then a furious creature raked its claws at me.

"Go," I commanded Tamara, and to my relief the snap of command worked. She dashed past me, through the space I'd cleared, as the rest of the pack descended on me.

Six-limbed, fast, and dangerous, the creatures stood waist high to me. But they were spindly things, built for speed not for battle. The first one thrashed on my spear, blood spraying as I spun to face its companions.

The next pounced straight at my face, claws slashing. They were wickedly long and sharp, but before they reached me, I smashed a punch into its spindly body. It tumbled back with a howl, others rushing in to replace it.

Pulling the spear free, I stabbed at the next one. The point wasn't sharp enough to penetrate its hide, but the impact drove it away.

The pack was all around me now, but none of them wanted to be first in. I'd killed one, injured another badly — none of the animals wanted to be the first to rush me. But there were too many of them for comfort. I'd certainly take some down, but if they came at me all at once I wouldn't stand a chance of winning.

Tamara was out of the trap. That was the main thing. The rest was details.

One of them edged closer, claws scrabbling at the dirt as it readied itself to rush me. I didn't give it the chance. Roaring a challenge, I braced my spear and charged, hoping to frighten them off. If I was too dangerous, they'd look for other prey.

But even as I leaped, I realized my mistake. Those claws weren't made for combat as much as they were for climbing, and as I lunged at the one who'd put himself in front of me, another dropped from the canopy above me. I turned, twisting and stabbing, and managing to strike the falling animal as it struck me.

Long, sharp claws scored my arms, missed my face by inches, sent blood spraying. The beast's weight drove it down on the spear, and the impact overbalanced me. Together, we tumbled to the floor, the rest of the pack closing in around me.

The spear fell from my hand, yanked by the weight of the dying creature. The others were too close for it now anyway. This would be a battle of claws and teeth and numbers.

I sliced the first throat to come near, kicked another animal in the face, and felt jaws close on my leg. Too many. *At least I die a warrior, saving my khara.*

With a yowl of pain, the jaws opened. Tamara shouted something, stabbing with her bloody spear, driving the creatures back. My heart swelled with pride at her warrior spirit even as I tried to tell her to run. What use was my sacrifice if she came back to die alongside me?

That means you can't die yet, I told myself, rolling to my feet as the pack adjusted to the new threat. *Get up, warrior, and save her.*

Tamara didn't know how to use her spear, and only the element of surprise had protected her this far. Her desperate stabs drove back the creatures in front of her, but others were circling and as soon as they had her surrounded, the fight would be over.

Not if I can help it, I thought, throwing myself back into the fray. The nearest of the climbing creatures fell under my claws, and I howled a challenge at the next. They scattered back, buying us time, and spared my khara a glance.

Uninjured, thank whatever gods watch over fools. "You should have run."

"And then what?" Tamara demanded. "How far would I get without you?"

There was an edge to her words, one I couldn't quite decode. This wasn't the time to worry about it, anyway. The creatures were spread out around us now, and I caught the rustle of leaves above us. Soon enough we'd be under attack again, and I didn't want to waste time arguing.

"When they attack, I will draw them to me," I said. It was the only plan I could think of if she refused to run. "You pick them off with the spear."

"That's a terrible plan," my khara said. "They'll kill you even if we win. I've got a better idea."

To my horror, she dropped her spear. I swore, ready for the creatures to take advantage of our sudden vulnerability. But even as they started their rush, Tamara's hand went to her bracelet, fingers dancing over the controls.

Her little hologram blinked into existence beside her, flickering as its mouth opened in a howl that rapidly rose in pitch until I couldn't hear it any more.

I might not be able to hear it, but the alien animals could. Screeching in pain and fear they scattered around us, one falling from the branches above as it tried to cover its ears with all of its limbs. I watched, astounded, as they fled into the underbrush.

Tamara slumped back against a tree, sinking down its trunk until she was sitting on the mossy ground. The hologram animal nuzzled against her hand as she reached out for it, and she muttered something encouraging to it.

"I didn't think that would work," she admitted after a moment. "I thought it would probably drive them mad again."

Around us the forest was in uproar as animals reacted to the ultrasound by fleeing. I looked around in wonder, then back to my khara.

"How did you know what sound to use?" I asked her, crouching next to her and looking down at the hologram that had saved our lives. It looked back almost smugly, and I couldn't help smiling. The little virtual pet had earned my thanks again.

"I guessed," Tamara said and grinned shakily and searching for the right words. "Mr. Mews recorded the creature last night."

That made sense. The predator's roar would have harmonics that scared the local animals, and if she'd managed to work that into the ultrasound I could see how that would work.

A huge gamble — it could just as easily have driven the predators into a frenzy. But given the danger, it had been a risk worth taking. And it had paid off.

I patted the hologram's translucent head, the faint force-field effect tingling under my fingers. Mr. Mews wriggled happily, lifelike enough to make me smile again. "We should not wait here though, they might come back. We need to get some distance from their territory before we camp."

Tamara didn't look happy about that but she didn't argue either. Pulling herself to her feet, she picked up her spear and we cautiously made our way away from the ambush site. Let the hunters find other prey.

Once we were well away from the wreck, I found a clearing where we could stop to open the pack I'd salvaged. It held the usual essentials: survival blankets for cold weather, nutrient bars, a simple inertial mapping system, a first aid kit — and most importantly of all, a communicator.

I whispered a prayer as I pressed the power switch. The emergency communicator was shielded, and maybe that would have kept it safe from whatever weapon had drained the power supplies.

No. Of course I couldn't be that lucky. I pressed the switch again, but there was no response. Whatever the taveshi had done, it was thorough.

"Let me see," Tamara said, taking the communicator out of my hands and turning it over, frowning. Pulling a tool from her belt she managed to pry open the casing and looked inside. A bright smile spread across her face as she worked.

She muttered something in her own language, taking off her armband and opening it to get at the circuits inside. The hologram cat vanished as she started to work on the internal circuitry that maintained it, and I frowned.

"Don't worry, Mr. Mews will be back," she told me, looking up. My frown deepened. It wasn't as though I was worried about the little virtual pet. Or at least, I wouldn't admit to it easily.

But I could see what she was doing, and it was a good idea. Her short-range communicator could use the emergency comm as an amplifier, and maybe she could get in touch with other human survivors.

Without satellites in orbit to relay the messages, it wouldn't be able to reach far. Still, it was much better than nothing — if she could get it to work. Leaving her to do her best, I patched my injuries with the first aid kit. Sprayskin sealed and disinfected the wounds; I would be left with impressive scars but nothing worse.

"Done," Tamara said eventually, triumph warring with fear in her voice. Not fear of failure, I realized. Fear of what she might find when she powered up the hybrid communicator.

At the moment we didn't know if there was anyone else broadcasting. Once she switched that on, we'd find out — and what would it mean if there were no signals? If no humans were calling out on the radio?

At the moment she had hope that the other humans had survived the *Wandering Star's* crash. As soon as she used that device, it could be ripped from her.

I walked to her, putting a hand on her shoulder.

"Tamara, we saw the colony pods launch," I

reminded her. "Even if there's no one in range, some of your people will have made it to the surface safely."

She didn't look convinced but she nodded anyway. With a quick, decisive motion she pressed the switch and static roared from the speakers. Tamara winced, dialing down the volume and searching through the frequencies.

On the hybrid system she'd set up that wasn't easy. Signals faded in and out as she adjusted the set up. Sometimes we heard the steady beeping of an automated call, other times a clear but empty channel. It took forever to find a voice.

When she did tune into one, my heart sank. I recognized that cold, smug voice, and it had no business on a human frequency. I'd hoped that I'd heard the last of it in orbit.

Of course I wouldn't be that lucky, I thought as Zaren spoke.

"— gather at the human ship," Zaren's voice crackled over the communicator. "Follow this signal to find it. Warriors of the Silver Band, rejoice. We have won a great victory. This world is ours!"

I resisted the urge to throw the device against the nearest tree. All of this and he'd still managed to win, to take the humans and their ship captive. Tamara's people would be enslaved at best, slaughtered at worst.

I hadn't saved them.

Tamara's hand touched my arm, startling me. She might not know the prytheen language Zaren spoke, but she could see the effect it was having on me and she offered me comfort without question.

I shrugged off her hand. How could I accept her sympathy when I'd failed her so badly?

"Auric, what's wrong?" She wasn't discouraged. Not yet.

"Zaren's alive," I told her. I didn't want to tell her, but she deserved to know. "He has the *Wandering Star*, and he's calling the rest of the Silver Band to him."

I expected her to recoil. But instead her eyes lit up.

"You don't understand," I said. "He's seized your ship, your people."

"No, *you* don't understand," she replied, grabbing my hand and squeezing. "I was afraid that they were all dead. If he's captured the ship, that means that there's a ship left to take. The colonists are still alive."

I blinked. That was a different, more hopeful way of looking at things. Not a realistic one, perhaps, but did that matter? A wild hope shone in Tamara's eyes as she continued.

"All we need to do is take the ship back," Tamara continued. I opened my mouth to protest, and Tamara put her hand over my mouth. "No, Auric. Don't argue. However impossible you say it is, it's easier than it would be if they were all dead."

I frowned, but I couldn't think of an argument. Alone against however many of the Silver Band warriors heeded Zaren's call? The odds were unthinkable. But not, strictly speaking, impossible. And since

I'd resigned myself to failure, our chances couldn't exactly get worse.

If I'm going to fail, I may as well do it gloriously.

Taking her hand, I looked Tamara in the eyes.

"You're right," I told her. "I will free your people or die trying."

15

TAMARA

*W*ith the radio signal to guide us, Auric calculated the direction to the *Wandering Star*. Zaren's words repeated over and over as Auric worked, and I hated listening to it. He wasn't speaking Galtrade so I couldn't understand a word of his little speech but there were a few things even I could tell from his tone.

First, he might claim he'd won a great victory but he didn't sound *happy*. If anything, he sounded angry. Second, there was a catch in his breathing. Had he been injured in the crash?

I hoped so. His attack had caused all this pain, killed so many of his followers and my crew. He deserved whatever suffering the crash had landed on his head.

"I have a course," Auric said at last. Focused on a task now, he was all business. That only made him more attractive somehow. His face a hard mask of determination, I saw the spark in his gaze as he looked to the horizon.

Toward the mountains that rose over the forest. Great.

"Are we going to have to climb those?" I asked dubiously. I'd done some climbing when I was younger. On an indoor wall. And I'd fallen off a lot.

To my relief Auric shook his head. "I doubt the signal would have carried through the mountains. Wherever the *Wandering Star* came down, it must be on this side. Probably in the foothills."

"Thank god," I muttered, looking at the peaks that rose like jagged teeth. They did *not* look like a fun outing.

The walk there would be challenging enough. I looked down at my feet and the soft shoes I wore. Intended for wearing aboard the ship, not for trekking through mud, they were already starting to come apart.

I had boots that would be perfect for this trip — locked away with my other possessions aboard the *Wandering Star* until we arrived at Arcadia.

Auric followed my look down and frowned. "We will set out tomorrow," he said in a tone that brooked no argument. "Today we rest up and prepare."

I wanted to argue, but honestly I was too tired to face a long march right now anyway. My muscles ached all over, my feet were sore, and I felt like I needed to sleep for a week.

Though how I'd be able to sleep while worrying about the tentacle-tiger from the night before, I had no idea. My arm still tingled from its venom and the idea of a monster like that creeping up on us was terrifying.

I need a better name for those things. A tenger? It'll do. Giving the monster a name made it a little less frightening somehow. I could pretend I understood the danger.

Auric set up another camp against a tree, and I lit a fire. This time it went a lot quicker — maybe I was getting the hang of it? The evening was drawing in by the time we'd finished, which seemed far too fast. I checked with Mr. Mews. Yep, this planet had a quick day-night cycle, only about twenty hours. Hopefully we wouldn't be here long enough to need to get used to that change.

Thinking about how long we might be here made me worry about Mr. Mews' battery. On the ship my wristband constantly charged, but out here I didn't know how long the battery would last. He wasn't supposed to be running the ultrasound constantly, and we had no way to replace his batteries until we reached the *Wandering Star*.

"Sorry, little friend," I said as I made a decision. "I'm going to have to make some changes."

Going into the settings, I turned off everything I could apart from the ultrasonics. The hologram vanished, and I tried not to feel like a traitor as he faded away.

I'll bring you back as soon as I can, I promised Mr. Mews silently. *This is just while we need your battery life.*

Even if the battery lasted, would this sound keep

back all of the local wildlife? Or were only some animals afraid of the tengers, leaving whatever else was here to eat us in our sleep? There was no way to tell except by trying it out.

I tried to put my faith in the way the whole forest had seemed to react to the ultrasound earlier.

The colony pods had their own ultrasonic fences, purpose-built to keep away wildlife. Maybe if we found one on our way to the mountains, we'd be able to get something like a safe camp set up. Once I'd updated the fences to send the right sound, that was. The default setting would not be good, and I shuddered to think what might have happened if any of the colonists had set them up without testing them.

Let's hope that no one's gotten themselves eaten.

"I will hunt us some food," Auric said, standing. "I recovered some emergency rations, but we should save those."

Picking up his spear, he turned toward the forest. I grabbed his wrist, instantly terrified to be left alone on this planet.

"Please stay."

He looked at me, and my cheeks warmed under his gaze. The sensation of his skin under my fingers, the warmth of his touch, it all made him feel more real. It wasn't that I'd forgotten the feeling of him, but I'd pushed it out of my mind.

It all rushed back in as we faced each other.

You hardly know him, part of me said. *And he's a killer, a predator.*

But the idea of being hunted by him didn't sound so bad. The intensity of those eyes on me, his strength, his amazing body. All of it called to me.

For a moment, I thought he'd pull free of my grip. I couldn't have held him if he wanted to go.

Instead, he dropped his spear and pushed me against a tree. I gasped at the casual strength with which he moved, looking up into his eyes and feeling a delicious shiver of fear and excitement run through me.

"Do not tempt me," he growled, voice low. Hungry. I saw his control slipping as he looked down at me, his hard body close enough that I felt the heat radiating from him.

I tried to speak. No words came out. I couldn't even think, let alone form a coherent sentence. The world faded around us, and Auric was everything. His scent filled my senses, a heady musk that made my pulse race as he leaned in.

My hand rose instinctively to block him, pushing against his chest. His heartbeat, strong and fast, pushed against me, and then he knocked my hand aside and leaned in to take the kiss we both wanted.

The touch of his lips on mine was electric, driving everything else from my mind. I couldn't breathe, couldn't think, couldn't do anything but cling to him and ride the wave of sensation he sent through me until at last we parted, panting.

His face inches from mine, Auric growled again. I whimpered softly, unable to even think of moving, and he lifted me with strong hands. Pressed me back against the trunk of the tree, my eyes level with his.

"You are mine," he said, and I wouldn't have argued if I could. His powerful, muscular body trapped me, and I nodded.

That was all the invitation he needed to tear my top open, burying his face in my neck and biting down. Sharp teeth dug into my skin hard enough to make me yelp and writhe and I felt him harden against me at the sound.

There was pain, but the wave of passion and pleasure that followed drowned it out. I grabbed at him, my hands in his hair, my back arching as I tried to keep some control over myself.

No chance of that. My body responded to his touch, burning with need and lust. I clung to him desperately, wanting him more than I'd ever wanted anything in my life. The illusion that I could resist this urge, resist *him*, vanished like morning mist. Auric's touch stripped that away, just as he stripped me of my clothes.

He set me down, naked and panting, his eyes shining as he looked at me. The careful focus as he examined me made me feel self-conscious again, but when I tried to cover myself with my hands, he grabbed my wrists and stopped me.

"You are mine," he said again. "And I wish to look at you."

My only response was a little whimper, and a blush spread across me as he stared. He stalked around me, his eyes raking my body, and I had never felt so exposed.

So helpless.

So *sexy*.

His desire for me was plain to see, and I could almost feel it. A pulsing need, an ache that we both shared, a fire that burned in his heart. There was no pretending that this was my imagination. Auric wanted me as much as I wanted him.

All that was holding him back was his willpower. And that was hanging by a thread.

I reached out for him, fingers trembling, and he nodded. Guided my hands to the fastening of his pants. They were unfamiliar and I fumbled at them for a frustrating moment before they opened, freeing his cock.

His magnificent, hard cock.

I gasped, staring, and Auric chuckled. Taking my hand he guided it, letting me feel the solid length of him. It wasn't just the size that was spectacular: it was unlike anything I'd seen before. The surface was covered in ridges and bumps, and as I stroked it, I felt it pulse.

My face bright red, I bit my lip and gripped firmer. The vibrations sped up, and I shivered at the thought of that inside me. *Yes please. Oh god yes.*

But for all his urgency, his need, Auric was in no hurry. His hands stroked up my arm, claws scratching gently over my skin, just hard enough to make me squirm. They traced a strange pattern across my neck, down my chest, over my breasts.

Every move he made sent a wave of desire through me, more powerful than anything I'd ever felt before. All the nerves in my body seemed to be tuned to Auric's touch, needing it, desperate for it. His fingers expertly caressed my body and slid down my sides.

Taking hold of my hips, he lifted me back into a kiss. Our naked bodies pressed together, and I cried out as he lowered us to the ground, pushing me down into the alien grass.

Auric was panting now too, the last strands of his self-control fraying as he kissed his way down my neck, down to my breasts. Sucking a nipple into his hot mouth, he flicked his tongue across it, making me cry out. My hand, still on his cock, tightened and I felt a buzz as it vibrated against me.

His hungry, eager moan sent a shudder through me, and I parted my legs eagerly as his hand stroked between them. Sharp claws traced over my inner thighs, teasingly close to the aching emptiness of my pussy, and I bit my lip as I arched. I wanted him, needed him, and hated having to wait.

But I'd get what I wanted when he decided. I knew that there was no arguing with that. And, infuriating as that was, it made me squirm to be so completely at Auric's mercy.

With delicate precision he slipped a finger between my folds, careful of his claws. I gasped as the pad of his thumb brushed my clit. Moaned as he rubbed, slowly at first then faster. Faster. My body shook, and I stroked his cock, matching the speed he set.

His breath came fast, panting, and he looked up at me. His eyes shone, radiant with lust and need and love, and he pressed down harder, sending a wave of pleasure through me. And another, and another. Each built on the last, each pushed me toward the edge of the climax I knew was coming.

I tried to speak, but all that came out were little gasps of joy. But he understood my need, grinning down at me. Lowering his mouth to my neck, he bit down, sending a final wave of pleasure through me and lifting me into an orgasm that shook my world.

I arched under him, crying out, my body shaking. For a moment there was nothing but *Auric*, his body, his fingers, his mouth. My mind melted into the waves of ecstasy and I clung to him.

"My god," I gasped when I could think again. "Auric, that was incredible."

I'd forgotten my Galtrade, but that didn't matter. Auric's broad grin made it clear that he understood what I was saying.

That hungry, eager smile made me shiver all over again, seeing the pride he took in pleasing me. And he wasn't done yet.

He slipped between my legs, his weight pinning me to the damp grass, and my heart hammered as his cock pressed against my pussy. My eager, aching pussy. *Oh god.*

I stroked his back, feeling the powerful muscles moving as he positioned himself. His golden, cat-like eyes looked down into mine, and I knew that my need was written plain across my face.

With a slow, deliberate motion Auric thrust. I felt every ridge of his alien cock as it slid into me, stretching me and filling me, making me arch and gasp and writhe. He didn't stop until he'd buried himself to the hilt. My body tightened around him, and he vibrated inside me, a sensation almost as strange as it was erotic.

I whimpered something, even I didn't know what, and he started to move again. Slowly he pulled back, leaving me achingly empty again for just a moment before he thrust again, harder. Driving me down into the ground, my mouth open in a gasp of pleasure.

Again, and again, he thrust. Each time harder, each time faster. My body shook as I clung to him, digging my nails in and urging him on and on. I could barely breathe under him as the pleasure built again, filling me, sending me wild with need.

Auric swelled inside me, his cock vibrating and growing, filling me perfectly with each powerful thrust.

Yes. Oh god yes!

I yelled out, a scream of pure pleasure as he brought me back to the edge of orgasm. For a moment I teetered on the brink, nearly-but-not-quite toppling into the waves of ecstasy — and then Auric lowered his mouth to bite down hard on my neck.

The sharp shock of that sent me tumbling away, my world disintegrating in wave after wave of pleasure. I felt him follow me over, roaring as he came, his cock quivering inside me as he came.

We shook together, clinging on to each other for a long time before finally collapsing in a panting mess. Auric groaned and pulled me to him as he rolled onto his back, and I rested my head on his chest while I tried to get my breath back.

My body ached, my throat was raw from shouting, and my every muscle trembled. And I felt fantastic. I could hear Auric's heart pounding every bit as fast as my own as he stroked my hair, one powerful hand gently on me.

He said something then, some word I didn't know. Whatever it was, it echoed in my soul and I smiled. It felt *right* in a way that I couldn't place.

"Khara," he said again, a little louder. "My khara, my Tamara."

Yes. I was his, and he was mine. Whatever we found when we reached the *Wandering Star*, we'd face it together.

～

IT WAS a good thing we had those emergency rations because Auric never did get to his hunt. We rested in each other's arms until well into the night before either of us could face moving. When I finally sat up and stretched, I grinned happily down at Auric, admiring his wonderful body. He opened his eyes to look up at me, smiling a little smugly.

He's earned it, I thought, feeling the happy ache in my muscles and flushing slightly. Stroking his chest I felt the warmth of his alien skin and sighed happily. There was a connection between us now, undeniable and strong, and I never wanted it to fade.

"My khara," he whispered.

"I don't know that word," I told him. My Galtrade vocabulary had grown a lot on this journey, but 'khara' had never come up. Whatever it meant, it made me smile.

His eyes met mine, gazing deep into me and making me blush all over. I could see him consider his words, carefully choosing what he would say as he reached up to stroke my cheek.

"It is a prytheen word," he told me at last, quiet and intense. "There is no word for it in Galtrade. It means the one to whom I will dedicate my life. The one I would live or die for. My mate, my soul, my heart. My khara."

I swallowed, not knowing how to respond to that declaration. What could I say? Anything seemed inadequate. In the end, I didn't answer with words, leaning in to kiss him on the lips. Auric pulled me to him, holding me tight, and in his arms I felt safer than I had in years.

Somehow I knew he meant what he said. He'd put himself between me and harm, shown that he was willing to die to protect me. The strength of his body, of his soul, was mine — and I realized that I felt the same way.

Everything that had happened since we'd met had been awful, but at least it had thrown us together.

When we separated at last, I bit my lip and tried to meet his powerful gaze. Brushed a finger across his lips. Took a deep breath and spoke.

"Khara," I said, tasting the word as it left my lips. Yes. It felt *real*. Auric's eyes gleamed as he nodded. "My khara."

I would have lain there forever with him if I could, but we had to move. Disentangling myself from my alien lover, I reached for my clothes only for Auric to take my arm gently but firmly and stop me.

I laughed. "Oh, I'm not allowed to get dressed now?"

"Not until I'm done looking at you."

Looking to the heavens, I mock-groaned. "I guess that's that, then. I'm going to be naked forever."

He laughed, delighted, and pulled me back to him. Falling against his chest I kissed him eagerly, feeling the strange and wonderful texture of his alien skin. *I could get used to this.*

I hope I have a chance to get used to it.

16

AURIC

The march into the foothills was long, but it was also pleasant. Protected from predators by the ultrasound, I could spare my attention for my companion.

I was with my khara, and we were on a mission together.

That the mission was hopeless didn't matter. It was still better than where we'd been before we had somewhere to go.

We fell into a pattern over the days of our journey. Walking for half the day, then scouting for a place to set up camp. I'd hunt while Tamara lit a fire, and then we'd cook what I caught. The ultrasound from her armband kept her safe while I hunted… and would for as long as the battery lasted. Then she'd be vulnerable again.

That wasn't the only worry. While I could find plenty of prey in the strange, alien forest, neither of us knew anything about these animals. Nor did we know if any of the plants were safe to eat. Sooner or later we were bound to either eat something toxic or find that our diet was missing vital nutrients. The emergency rations we'd found helped with that, but we couldn't rely on them. For one thing, they were prytheen rations — for all I knew they were missing something Tamara needed to survive.

Another reason to get to the ship with its food stores.

Despite the dangers, there was something viscerally satisfying about hunting to feed my mate. It was a pleasure I'd never experienced, and one I came to treasure.

There were plenty of other pleasures for us to share, too. We had to be careful to leave enough time for sleep.

It was almost a shame when we reached the hills where the ship had come down. Our journey was nearing its end, and I expected that the end would be final. We would be facing a fortified position. And there were only the two of us, armed with fire-hardened spears, against however many prytheen had gathered to follow Zaren in his conquest.

We hadn't discussed tactics. I didn't want to worry Tamara, and she didn't seem to want to think about it. Besides, there was little we could decide before we saw what we were up against.

Now that we were nearly there, though, I had to make some decisions. And that meant gathering more information. The *Wandering Star* had come down near here, and I thought it would be visible from the high ground. But taking my khara on a scouting mission? No. Far too dangerous for me to risk.

"I will climb the hill and see the lay of the land," I told my mate. "You stay back here."

"But—"

I cut off her protest. "No. I am a trained warrior and a hunter. I can approach unseen where you would draw the eyes of sentries. And there *will* be sentries, Zaren is no fool."

Tamara glared, but there wasn't much she could say to argue. While the days of travel had toughened her up, she hadn't picked up enough woodcraft to avoid being spotted.

"Fine," she said, throwing up her arms. "I guess I stay here and get eaten by tengers while you're scouting."

I smiled but shook my head. "Your ultrasound will protect you from the wildlife while I'm away, just like when I'm hunting."

"And what then? I just sit here until you've gone in and gotten yourself killed?"

"No." I reached out and squeezed her shoulder. "No, my khara. I will find a place from which we can observe in safety, then return and fetch you. I would not abandon you."

She frowned, then looked at the ground. "I know that, Auric. It's just hard to really believe it, when that means waiting here on my own."

I drew her to me, holding her tight. Breathing in

her scent deeply. "I would never abandon you. I could not if I tried."

She melted against me, but I could tell she wasn't convinced. Not fully. *I shall just have to prove it to her.*

Kissing her gently, I released her and stepped back into the strange forest. The sooner I found a place to watch from, the quicker I could be back at my khara's side.

The hill was steep, rough terrain to climb. And worse if I wanted to keep quiet, which I had to. Zaren's men would be listening as well as watching. It took me hours to climb to the top of the hill, guided by the smell of smoke from beyond it.

Gray rocks rose from the ground at the top of the hill, and the trees nearby had been flattened. Splinters lay everywhere, as I approached the crest and, hiding myself amongst the rocks, looked over into the valley beyond.

There I saw a scene of utter devastation. Whoever had been at the helm of the *Wandering Star* had managed a nearly miraculous landing, but that hadn't been enough to make it *neat*.

The giant ship had plowed into the ground between two hills, scattering earth and rocks and bits of ship everywhere. The impact had knocked over every tree in sight. It must have come in slow, because the ship was still mostly in one piece, but the damage was extensive. Getting it spaceworthy would take a lot of work that I doubted could be done on this planet.

The hull was torn open on one side and half the

superstructure had crumpled. The drive section looked bent. And the prow of the ship was buried in the hill. It was no longer a ship so much as a building.

But it had been designed for that possibility. This was a colony ship, intended to become the heart of the community. Even after this rough a landing it was still functional as a base, and I could see the telltale shimmer of the forcefield in the air. It was safe from the predatory wildlife, which would be worth a lot to any colony.

This would make a good base for the survivors of the crash if there were enough of us.

I frowned at that thought. Of *us?* When had I started to think of myself as part of whatever community formed here?

An image of Tamara flashed into my mind, and I knew. It had happened when I accepted that she was my khara and our fates were intertwined. If she couldn't get back to Earth and her people there, then this planet would have to be our home.

I would make it a good one.

Below, around the ship, figures moved. Wishing I had binoculars, I tried to make out what was happening. Humans, I thought. Humans digging at the prow of the ship, excavating some of the sensor pods which had been buried in the crash.

For a moment I hoped that meant the humans had regained control of the ship. But no, standing back from the work party I saw the taller, bulkier forms of prytheen warriors. Three of them, watching the humans work.

One of the humans stumbled and fell, and a prytheen was on him instantly, lashing him with a whip until he screamed loud enough for me to hear at this distance. My hands tensed on the rock, and I fought down the urge to rush to his rescue. I had to be smarter than that — one of the warriors held a rifle, and I had no hope of crossing the distance between us without being seen and shot.

So this is how low the Silver Band has fallen, I thought. *Slavery of weaker races.*

It was like something out of the tales of our distant past, the horrors the Code had been written to escape. We only fight equals. Treat defeated foes with respect and dignity. Turn our hands to the work that needs doing.

Below me I saw the results of Zaren's turning from that path. He sought to be the Alpha-of-Alphas, the ruler of us all, and seeking that he'd break every part of the Code if it helped him.

This will not stand. I promised myself that, and I knew that even if I failed, Zaren's reign wouldn't last long. Unbound by the Code, his followers would turn on him soon enough. Dishonorable leaders made for dishonorable followers, ones that would seize their moment to depose their alphas.

However short his reign was, though, it would be hell for the humans who had to suffer through it. As another alpha of the Silver Band, it was my obligation to stop that from happening.

In theory I had as much authority over the Band as Zaren. In practice, he'd built up far more support than I had amongst the warriors of the Band. At the time I'd put that down to his successes in battle and raiding.

Now I had begun to wonder how he'd been so successful. Whether he'd ignored the Code and struck at unlawful targets, getting rich off the suffering of the weak rather than using his power to protect them.

It didn't matter how he'd gotten this far, though. Here we were, and now he had let go of the honorable ways of war to install himself as Alpha-of-Alphas.

As I watched, another group of prytheen approached from the north. Three of them, cautious and careful, making their approach obvious. They didn't want to be seen as a threat.

I recognized one of them, a lieutenant in Terasi's clan. No friends of Zaren, usually. I wondered how they'd be greeted.

Warriors hurried out to meet them, and I could see the tension in the trio of newcomers. They looked hungry, tired from their trek and nervous about this meeting. But the warriors from the *Wandering Star* greeted them as old friends, with warm embraces and gifts of food.

Yes, that would be effective, I judged. Who could say no to food when they were starving? A warrior might face death in battle without fear or pause.

Hunger was a harder foe to stare down, and not every warrior was a hunter.

Soon they were all moving back to the ship, and I knew that Zaren had three new warriors. Bribes of stolen food to buy the loyalty of hungry warriors who couldn't hunt their own meals.

How far have we fallen? I shook my head at that. Zaren was gathering the weaker members of the Silver Band to himself, that was all. The stronger hunters would serve other alphas and keep to themselves. There might be any number of clans forming elsewhere on the planet. Some of them, perhaps even most, would follow the Code.

But if Zaren could gather enough warriors into an army, he would be able to bring down the other alphas with raw numbers. With the *Wandering Star* as a base he had the strongest position, and his boundless ambition would be the death of honor on this planet.

Even if he lost, he could kill all hope of survival for the humans. My khara's people would suffer and die for Zaren's dreams of conquest unless I stopped him somehow. That uncomfortable thought filled my mind as I crept back towards the tree line, and my Tamara.

Together, we'd come up with a plan.

17

TAMARA

With Auric gone the forest felt dangerous. No, *more* dangerous — it had never felt safe, even with him at my side. Huddling in a small clearing, my back to a tree, I waited for him to return.

The eerie silence of the forest just made it easier to imagine all kinds of monsters creeping up on me, and I clutched my spear tight. Would it actually help if something came hunting me? I didn't know, but I wasn't about to let myself get taken without a fight no matter what.

I had to hope that the ultrasound my wristband was putting out would keep any predators at bay. Unfortunately, there wasn't any way of testing that apart from waiting for something to try to kill me. Maybe the silence meant it was working and all the animals were avoiding me. I hoped so.

I wish I could speak to Mr. Mews. If I couldn't have Auric with me, at least the virtual cat would be some company. But I couldn't risk the battery drain of switching him back on.

Somewhere in the woods a twig snapped. My head whipped round to look where that had come from, but I couldn't see anything through the thick undergrowth. That was, of course, the point. I was in a hidden dell, out of sight of any passing hunters.

Taking deep breaths, I tried to keep still and silent, listening intently. Voices, hushed and low, carried on the breeze. Voices speaking a language I didn't know but recognized as prytheen.

Wonderful, some of Auric's comrades were here. Far too close for comfort. I hoped that they'd miss me and pass on by.

"Let go of me!"

The English words startled me, and I bit back a gasp. That was a male voice, one I didn't recognize — but then again, I didn't know any of the colonists. I could hardly imagine what it must be like for them, waking from stasis on the wrong planet and being captured by aliens.

A prytheen laughed coldly and I heard the meaty sound of a slap. The human cried out in pain, other voices joining his protests. I winced, unable to resist creeping closer. While the prytheen might have better senses than humans, their captive was distracting them, and that gave me a chance to get a look at what was happening.

Parting the purple undergrowth, I watched a ragged group marching by. Two prytheen and four humans, the humans leading the way and pushing through the brush. They wore the green jumpsuits of the Arcadia colonists and they looked confused, frightened, desperate. The prytheen laughed amongst themselves as they drove their captives on.

The aliens didn't look too well, either. In fact, they looked worse off than their prisoners. Wherever they'd crashed, it hadn't gone as well for them as our landing had — both were injured, one with a blood-stained bandage around his head, the other limping along using a metal spar as a crude crutch.

Despite their wounds they were still clearly in charge, driving the prisoners on. The humans... they looked like a family, parents and their teenager children, a son and a daughter. Bruised and battered, they still looked healthy, but I doubted that would last long.

The son had tried to put up a fight, it looked like, and one of the prytheen held him pinned to a tree by his throat, his face darkening as he scrabbled helplessly at the alien's hand.

The other alien held the rest of the family at bay as they tried to help. Unarmed, even with the weight of numbers they couldn't hope to do anything. Even injured, the prytheen were still warriors, still killers, and the colonists weren't.

Neither was I, but I had a weapon. I had the element of surprise. And I had a duty to protect the colonists. I was crew and that meant that I was supposed to keep the colonists safe until they reached Arcadia.

If that ever happens, I thought. It seemed like a

distant dream now, but I couldn't ignore their suffering.

"Leave him alone," I shouted in my crude Galtrade, stepping out of the undergrowth and brandishing my spear. The prytheen warriors turned to me, surprised, and for a moment I had the advantage. I knew it would be my only chance.

I lunged, aiming for the one with the head wound. If I could even the odds quickly, I might manage to win this fight.

My spear tip nearly reached his throat before he reacted, twisting aside and dropping the colonist. The spear missed by inches and he bared his teeth in an eager snarl. A clawed hand swiped at me, forcing me back as I ducked out of the way.

No, it wasn't going to be that easy.

"This human has teeth," Crutches chuckled, switching to Galtrade. Maybe he thought it would intimidate me, but all it did was piss me off.

"Cowards," I spat at him, glad I'd built up my vocabulary over days with Auric. He'd had plenty to say about his former comrades on our journey. "You attack the weak; try someone who can fight back."

Behind them, the colonists helped their injured son to his feet and looked around uncertainly. I hissed at the aliens, doing my best impression of an angry cat. Anything to keep their focus on me and off the helpless family.

What I'd do next, I didn't know. Keep them busy

while the others escaped? *Great plan, Tamara. What then?*

The one with the head wound darted forward, grabbing for the spear, and it was all I could do to keep it out of his hands. I ducked back, stabbed, and the tip caught him in the forearm.

It glanced off. Fire-hardened wood wasn't going to cut deep, not unless I landed a perfect hit.

The alien laughed, his comrade stalking around me. I looked between them, keeping the spear moving.

"Two against one?" I tried to laugh but my mouth was too dry. It came out more like a croak. "What honorable warriors you are."

A look of rage flashed across the face of Crutches, and he snarled something in his own language. I smiled as sweetly as I could, feinted in his direction, then swung the spear like a club at his friend.

The wooden shaft connected with a dull *thwack* but before I could follow it up, they were on me. Crutches swept my legs out from under me and Head-Wound pounced, pinning me to the ground with his weight. As quick as it had started, the fight was over. I'd lost.

"You will make a fine prize," the injured prytheen said, his face inches from mine. I growled and snapped my head forward, slamming into his nose and sending him reeling back howling.

Sensitive nose, check, I thought, scrambling for a weapon. The other warrior slammed his crutch down on my arm with bruising force, driving me away from my weapon.

And then the others rushed him. Rather than fleeing as I'd hoped, they'd come to my aid. I was caught between gratitude and frustration — what was the *point* of me helping them get away if they didn't run?

A small part of me spotted the irony. *This must be how Auric felt when I came back to help him.*

The four colonists hit the injured prytheen warrior at once, a tidal wave of humanity that carried him to the ground and let me grab my spear. Their weight was enough to hold him down and the father smashed at his head with a rock.

I didn't have time to watch, not with Head-Wound rushing me. He charged in blindly, roaring as he came. In desperation I dragged the spear up, bracing it against the ground as the prytheen warrior pounced.

His weight hit the spear tip before he could react, and with a wet squelch it buried itself in his belly. Clawed hands swung weakly at me as I dropped the weapon and backed away.

He tried to follow, but only made it a couple of steps before falling to his knees. Looking at me, he cursed and struggled weakly to pull the spear from his body.

It seemed to take forever for him to sink to the ground and stop moving. I couldn't tear my eyes away. That was the first time I'd killed, and as awful as the prytheen had been, it still felt terrible. That I'd had no choice didn't make it feel any better.

I wonder how Auric deals with this, I thought distantly

as the light went out in the eyes of my enemy. Finally I could look away.

"Thank you," the father of the family said, panting as he dropped the bloody stone he was carrying. He looked like he had a thousand questions but settled for just one. "What the hell is going on?"

His family clustered around him, looking horrified at what they'd done. They were no more prepared to kill than I was. Pulling myself to my feet, I looked at the alien bodies. Swallowed, wiped my hands on my pants, and shook my head.

"We have to get moving," I said. "I'll explain on the way, but we can't be here when the next lot of aliens come by."

The father looked like he was about to demand answers now, but his wife put her hand on his shoulder. He took a deep breath and nodded. "Okay, you're right. Where do we go?"

Good question. My little hidden camp was no good, it was far too close to the site of the fight. Up the hill, after Auric? But if he'd been right about there being sentries, the five of us would just run into them. In fact, they might have heard the fight and already be on their way here. *Crap.*

"Let's start with *away*," I decided, anxious to be on the move. "We can figure out where we're headed to later, but we can't stay."

I stole a glance back at the small clearing and my heart sank. That was where Auric would expect to find me when he returned, and if I wasn't there who knew what he would think. I couldn't even leave a clear trail for him to follow — if he could track me then so could any of the other prytheen.

But I couldn't stay there and gamble that he'd get here first. Not with the luck that I'd had lately. *I'll just have to trust to fate,* I decided. *It brought us together once, it'll do it again. It has to.*

Turning my back, I led the colonists into the woods and away from the hill. We had to get some distance before the prytheen started looking for us.

∼

"I'M CHRIS," the father told me once we'd walked far enough to put some distance between us and any pursuit. He still spoke quietly, as though frightened of being overheard. "Chris Martins. This is my wife, Abby, and our kids Maxine and Finn."

"Tamara Joyce," I answered, just as quietly. We'd heard no sign of pursuit but none of us wanted to take chances. "I'd say I'm pleased to meet you, but under the circumstances I don't know that's quite right."

Chris managed a laugh at that, but it sounded forced.

"You're crew, right? What happened? Where are we?" He got a hold of himself with a visible effort, shutting off the firehose of questions. But behind him, his family looked like they were about to add to them.

"Yes," I answered hurriedly, trying to get a word in before the deluge. "I'm the *Wandering Star's* engineer. I don't know where we are, though. The prytheen attacked us and we tried to escape, but we all crashed here. All I know is that we crashed on a world in the Tavesh Empire."

The family exchanged glances, and then Abby took up the questioning. "Can we get home? I mean, either Earth or Arcadia would do. We're not picky."

She tried to put a note of humor into that, but it fell flat. I sighed, shrugged, pushed my way deeper into the foliage. "I'd have to see the *Wandering Star* to know for sure, but it's not going to be easy. The last time I saw her, she was coming down hard — if we're lucky the pilot put her down carefully, but if not…"

I let that trail off, thinking about McKenzie and how little faith I'd had in his skills. Even a great pilot would have had difficulty with this one, and McKenzie had never struck me as a great *anything.*

He managed to get the colony pods down safely, I reminded myself. *Maybe I owe him an apology.*

No point in scaring the colonists, anyway. Maybe the ship could fly, maybe not: that wasn't the important question right now. Whatever condition the *Wandering Star* was in, there was a more fundamental issue.

"The real problem is that the prytheen have set up their camp at the ship," I told them. "That's where they were taking you, I think. Can you tell me what happened to you?"

Chris and Abby exchanged looks and then shrugged.

"We don't really know much," Chris said. "When the

stasis tubes opened we were already on the planet, and our colony pod was a mess. The autopilot landed us in one piece, but there's no chance the pod will fly again. I don't know how much of our equipment is salvageable — we were just starting to look at it when those two aliens showed up."

"At first we thought that they might be friends," Abby continued, her face hardening. "That lasted until they got in arms' reach of Maxine. One of them grabbed her, threatened to tear her throat out if we didn't do what they said. They checked the radio, heard a message we couldn't understand, and then dragged us off. You know the rest."

The anger in her expression made me shiver, and I was glad she was on my side. After the prytheen threatened Abby's children it was no wonder she'd been willing to attack them with rocks.

I wondered what the aliens wanted the colonists for. Given that they'd gathered them by force, I doubted it would be anything good.

"The rest of the colony pods," Maxine asked, frowning. "Did they get down okay?"

"I think so," I told her. "They're designed to find their own way down to a planet. I think they'll have landed as safely as yours, for what that's worth."

"Not much," the teenager said glumly. "Ours is a wreck. Everything we own is trash, and we're stuck here in this…"

She trailed off, hugging herself and shivering. I tried to imagine what things must be like from her point of view — whatever adventure she'd thought she was going on, she'd woken into a nightmare and been kidnapped by monsters. I couldn't blame her for being upset.

"Maybe some of your supplies are salvageable," I said. "We won't be able to last long out here without them. And you never know, maybe I can repair it. Do you think you can find your way back to the pod?"

Abby blinked. "Sure, I'm pretty good at directions and the crash site isn't hard to spot. Won't they look for us there, though?"

The anger in her voice left no doubt who she meant.

"I don't think we can afford to worry about that," Chris said, looking around and sighing. "We need equipment if we're going to do any hunting, or defend ourselves. We won't stay there, just grab what we can and go."

Finn had been quiet up till now, but he grinned at that.

"And maybe we can get the rover out," he said excitedly. Everyone else perked up at that, even me.

Each of the colony pods came equipped with an all-terrain vehicle, and after days trekking through the forest on foot I liked the idea of driving instead. It would be faster, more comfortable, and let us carry a lot more gear.

That settled it. We needed a destination, and the promise of a vehicle made the colony pod the best option. The only alternative I could think of would be to retrace my steps to the last camp Auric and I had used. Which would be comforting, and might let Auric find us, but it didn't offer any other advantages.

Abby took the lead and I followed, trying to think ahead and hoping that, somehow, Auric would find me again.

18

AURIC

I knew something was wrong as soon as I started my way down to Tamara. Something itched at the back of my skull, an instinct telling me all wasn't well with my khara. She was in danger, and I wasn't there to protect her.

I tried to tell myself that it wasn't real, that it was just nerves from being separated. She would be fine. I would return to her side and laugh at myself for worrying.

Then I smelled blood on the wind, and that pleasant fantasy evaporated. I fought down the urge to run. If something had happened to Tamara while I was away, I couldn't risk running into an ambush. I needed to live long enough to rescue her.

She wasn't alone, that much I could be sure of. I smelled both human and prytheen blood, the scents clear and distinct. They filled my senses, driving me wild with fear for my khara, but I forced myself to approach slowly and carefully.

Dead or captured I'd be no use to her. As much as it pained me, I had to be cautious.

The tiny hollow where I'd left her was empty, but just beyond it I found the remains of a fight. Two prytheen warriors I didn't recognize, both dead. One bludgeoned with rocks, the other impaled on Tamara's spear.

No human bodies. I relaxed slightly at that, letting out a breath and allowing myself to smile. Whatever had happened here, Tamara had survived it. That gave me hope. But my heart still hammered in my chest as I tried to piece things together.

There were human tracks alongside the prytheen, more than just Tamara's. At least three more, I judged, maybe four. The tracks vanished into the undergrowth and I lost sight of them quickly. Whoever was with Tamara, they knew how to hide their trail reasonably well.

Unfortunately, that didn't matter as much as the humans might think. The scent of blood was clear and easy to follow, and I set out along their course.

Worse news came quickly: I wasn't the only one on the hunt. Other prytheen were ahead of me, following the humans' trail. I bit back a snarl and moved faster, hoping that I could catch up with the hunters before they reached my khara.

I didn't want to think about what would happen if I

didn't. She'd killed prytheen warriors — Zaren wouldn't be merciful.

The woods seemed to close in around me as I raced after the humans and the prytheen who chased them. It didn't take long to close the distance, and soon I heard the hunters moving through the underbrush. They made no attempt to be stealthy. Why would they? They had no reason to think anyone was following them.

By the time I got close, they were hot on the humans' trail. Four of them at least, moving through the undergrowth quickly and quietly. And, worst of all, in a loose group.

Too close together to pick them off one by one. Too far apart to hit them all while I still had the element of surprise. I could take any one of them in a fight, I was confident. Two, probably.

Three would be pushing my luck. But four? Too many.

It didn't look like I'd have any choice but to risk it. Tamara and her human companions were close, and the prytheen would attack them soon. I had to make my move before that happened.

Ahead, the forest came to an abrupt end, the shattered remains of trees littering the ground where a crashing colony pod had tumbled to rest. I cursed. Once we left the trees, I'd have no cover. This was it, my last chance to pounce.

I wasn't ready, but it would have to do.

The humans were halfway across the broken

ground, making for the fallen colony pod. Their hunters paused at the forest's edge, laughing at the humans' attempt to flee, one of them speaking into a communicator as I closed the distance as quietly as I could.

"Now," he said, a savage hunter's joy in his voice. "The prey is in a clearing."

A boom split the sky as a transport ship zoomed overhead, circling and slowing, coming back around. I ducked back behind a tree, cursing my luck and their cowardice. These hunters didn't even have the guts to chase down the humans by themselves.

As I watched, the humans turned for the far side of the clearing, abandoning the colony pod and trying to get to cover. The transport dipped down, cargo ramp lowering, and from inside shots rang out. They burned across the path of the fleeing humans, forcing them to stop.

The transport was a human design, low tech by prytheen standards. Primitive enough that the taveshi weapon hadn't disabled it along with our ships. The guns, too, were human weapons rather than the blasters my people used. That was no comfort: they were still deadly enough to kill my khara if she resisted.

At least they weren't shooting to kill. The hunters wanted Tamara and the others alive, at least for now.

I gritted my teeth and thought. Stepping out into the open would be suicide — fighting the four hunters I'd been chasing would have been dangerous enough.

Now I faced the crew of that stolen transport too, and they had guns. Dying wouldn't help Tamara.

But I couldn't abandon her to the mercy of Zaren and his thugs either. I needed a plan, some way to come to her rescue.

While I tried to think, Tamara grabbed a stone and threw it at the hovering ship. A futile gesture born of desperation, but she wasn't giving in and I drew strength from that. I felt her fear and her frustration, and wanted nothing more than to join her, to fight off these attackers and see her safe.

All I had was my spear. To protect her I had to keep my emotions under control and pick the right moment for my attack. Carefully, slowly, I moved forward, keeping to the trees and staying out of sight. A mad plan formed in my mind, one that I should have rejected out of hand.

But I had nothing better to try.

The hunters left the forest, spreading out and stalking towards the humans as the transport settled to the ground. Hands raised in surrender, the humans stumbled towards the ramp. The prytheen hunters laughed gleefully, cruelly, and I knew whatever fate they had in mind for my beloved and her friends would be terrible.

I would not allow my khara to suffer. Charging to my death wouldn't protect her, so I had to wait. Wait, and do something extraordinarily stupid.

If it works it's not stupid, I told myself. *And if it doesn't work, I'll be too dead to feel ashamed of my failure.*

At the top of the ramp, Tamara turned to look back at the forest and looked right at me as though she knew I was there. I saw terror in her eyes, and under it a grim determination. She'd done what she could to help these humans, and she would keep doing that until she could help no more.

I would do no less for her.

The ramp snapped shut and the small ship's engines whined as it lifted off the ground. This was the chance I'd been waiting for, the only chance I'd have. Dropping my spear, I sprinted across the open space, closing the distance in long, fast bounds before pouncing.

My fingers caught a rail on the ship's undercarriage. It creaked under my weight, bent, and for a moment I thought it might snap. But no, it held, and as the ground fell away beneath me, I pulled myself up.

Clinging to the bottom of the transport, I tried to come up with a next stage to this mad plan. Despite the peril, my heart was at peace. Whatever danger Tamara was going into, I would be there to protect her.

That would have to be enough.

19

TAMARA

I felt Auric's eyes on me, or imagined that I did. Was he really out there in the woods, watching? Almost close enough to reach, and impossibly far away.

Hopefully it was all in my mind, and he was far away and safe. If he was here... I hated to think what he might do. Because even he couldn't save us, not from so many armed guards. At best he'd take some of them down with him while they killed him.

And that was the only thing that would make this day worse.

Auric, if you're out there, stay safe. Stay away. Don't take any chances for me. I thought that as intently as I could, hoping he'd somehow hear me. That he'd know to keep away. There was no point in both of us dying.

The flyer's ramp slammed shut behind me and the Martins, and the transport lifted off with a whine. I recognized it as one of the *Wandering Star's* cargo shuttles, which at least meant the ship had come down somewhat intact. I tried to take comfort from that, but it wasn't easy when these bastards had their hands on it.

The guns the prytheen carried were from the ship's armory too. While the Silver Band's technology had failed, they seemed to have no trouble stealing our gear and making do.

We rose unsteadily, the pilot cursing as he fought for control. The transport pulled to the side, brushing the trees, and for a moment I thought it might crash, giving us another chance to escape. No such luck. With a snarled stream of profanity, the pilot got us above the trees on course.

We sat in miserable silence, and I couldn't help wondering if I'd made a mistake in trying to rescue the Martins. It hadn't helped them: they were still prisoners and if anything, they were worse off now.

No. Perhaps I'd only put off the inevitable, but I *had* done that. And Finn would have died if I hadn't stepped in.

I tried to hold onto that as a victory, rather than worry about our future. It wasn't easy.

Almost before I knew it the transport pitched downward, coming in to land. When the ship settled again and the ramp lowered, we were on the familiar deck of the *Wandering Star*. The glossy black surface tilted at an uncomfortable angle beneath our feet as we stepped out to face our captors.

Around us stood dozens of prytheen warriors,

hands on their weapons. Beyond them humans gathered in huddled groups, colonists thawed from their stasis pods and forced to work. They cast frightened glances our way, and I realized our captors intended to make an example of us. To show their slaves what happens to humans who resisted the prytheen.

Directly ahead of us stood Zaren, glowering at us with sadistic rage. He looked tired, and he'd lost the smug grin I remembered. The sullen anger in his eyes didn't bode well for us.

I met his gaze steadily. If this was going to be my end, I would at least face my fate head on.

"So you're the humans who dared kill my men," Zaren said almost conversationally. His voice echoed across the deck. "Your deaths will be a lesson to the other humans. Slow and painful enough to discourage rebellion."

"I thought you assholes believed in honorable combat," I snapped. Probably not the best strategy, but I couldn't keep quiet. "First you attack an unarmed colony ship, then you kidnap a family of colonists, and now you're pissed off that we fought back and killed a couple of your thugs? Where's the honor in that?"

My face flushed and the words flew out of me. I finally had the chance to shout at the man who'd caused all of this, and I wasn't going to pass it up.

What was he going to do about it? Kill me twice?

The aliens looked shocked that I'd dare speak to their leader like that, and his blue face darkened with rage. Stepping forward to tower over me, he snarled.

"You aren't worthy of an honorable war. You are weak, prey for the strong to take if we want."

I should have been terrified. No, I *was* terrified, but a wave of anger buried my fear. If I'd stopped to think I'd have collapsed, cried, hidden. But I didn't give myself a moment — instead, I prodded Zaren in the chest with my finger and glared up at him.

"That's stupid, hypocritical, and cowardly." The prytheen alpha reared back at that, outraged. I carried on before he had a chance to interrupt. "You attacked us. We fought back and killed your men. You can't say we're weak and there for the taking *and* be angry when we prove you wrong."

We were straining my Galtrade vocabulary, and I knew I wasn't getting everything across. It was enough though — the prytheen warriors around us muttered and exchanged looks. Some outraged, some amused, a few guilty.

Making Zaren angry might not be the smartest thing I'd done, but what choice did I have? Backing down would just prove him right. Maybe if I got him angry enough, he'd kill me *quickly*.

An odd thing to hope for, maybe, but there was no fighting the inevitable. We were inside the *Wandering Star's* forcefield now. I heard its hum, saw the shimmer where the air crossed it. With Auric trapped outside, he couldn't save me. A quick death might be my best option.

Zaren laughed, a forced and unconvincing sound. He hadn't expected this reaction, not from a human.

"You think that just because you can kill two injured warriors in an ambush, you can call yourself my equal?" He laughed again, louder. "You are mistaken, little human, and I will show you all just what happens to humans who dare to challenge the might of the Silver Band."

My laugh was no more genuine than his. "If it's right to pounce on the weak and take from them, then what have I done wrong? They weren't strong enough to stop me."

His face twitched, anger flaring in his golden eyes. With a hiss, he raised a clawed hand high.

Don't show fear, don't show fear, don't show fear.

I tried to remember Auric's strength, to copy his confidence. Putting my hands on my hips I smiled, baring my teeth and looking at Zaren's throat. I doubted I could intimidate him, but there was no reason not to try.

If he was going to kill me where I stood, at least I'd go out looking tough.

One of the other prytheen laughed and said something. I had no idea what, but Zaren didn't like it. Turning and snapping at the others, he looked like he was at the end of his tether.

I took a guess at what they were arguing about and ran with it. With nothing to lose, I might as well try a desperation play.

"What's the matter?" I asked. "Your men not happy with the way you've led them? You've stranded them on this planet, you're all trapped here just like us. What a great alpha they've picked."

There's a certain feeling when you catch the mood of a crowd. I felt it like the prickling on my skin in the moments before a storm. Everyone's attention was on me as I said what they'd been feeling, and for a moment I thought I might get some of the aliens on my side.

Zaren backhanded me. He struck faster than I could react, and by the time I realized he was attacking I was lying on the deck. My jaw ached and the coppery taste of blood filled my mouth. I could barely move.

Towering over me, the alien alpha snarled. His claws slid out as he raised a hand over me, and I saw my death in his eyes.

I glared back, struggling to sit up. *Not going to lie back and take it,* I told myself, though the world seemed to spin around me.

Zaren's clawed hand slashed down towards my throat, only for another alien to grab his wrist. The shouting match started up again as Zaren pulled free, but it seemed that his authority wasn't absolute anymore.

While the aliens were distracted, Chris grabbed my arm and pulled me away from them. The other humans watched, looking at me with a mixture of fear and awe, and I swallowed, wondering if I'd doomed us all. Zaren might well be the type to kill everyone who'd seen his moment of weakness.

I worked my jaw, happy to find that it was only bruised rather than broken. "You shouldn't stand near me," I whispered to Chris. "If Zaren decides to kill me—"

"—he'll have to go through us," Abby said firmly. Chris nodded.

"You saved us, and you stood up to those alien bastards," he agreed. "The least we can do is back you up now."

I wanted to tell them to keep safely away from me, but the words wouldn't come. Instead I hugged Abby and hoped for the best.

The look on Zaren's face when he turned to face me told me I should prepare for the worst instead. The argument amongst the aliens had turned into a glaring standoff, but the ones backing Zaren outnumbered those who didn't.

I did my best, I thought, wishing it had been enough and hoping that my friends didn't get caught in the consequences.

Zaren didn't even speak to me. Didn't need to — the murderous rage in his expression told me enough. I'd pissed him off and embarrassed him, and I wouldn't survive that.

If he was going to kill me — and I knew he was — then at least his followers would remember me. They watched, uncomfortable, as their leader stalked forward to kill a helpless woman.

"Stop!" The shout echoed across the deck, and all the aliens turned to see who dared interrupt them. Even Zaren turned, a curse dying on his lips as he saw who'd spoken.

There, somehow, stood Auric. He stood next to the transport I'd arrived in, right in the heart of Zaren's territory with no explanation for his sudden appearance, and the other aliens seemed as surprised as I was.

Somehow, he'd managed to get through the forcefield. Somehow, he was here to save me.

My heart skipped a beat and I didn't know whether to laugh or cry. To save me, Auric had worked a miracle and delivered himself into Zaren's hands, and doomed himself. *You idiot,* I wanted to shout at him. *I wanted you to live.*

But he'd made his choice, rather than watching me die. And I knew I'd have done the same in his place — if he was an idiot, then so was I.

He strode towards me with perfect confidence, the other aliens parting around him. Auric kept his eyes on me, smiling as though he was perfectly safe. As though the other prytheen *weren't* staring at him with rage in their eyes, gripping for the blades at their belts.

The only hint of the pressure he was under was the careful, precise measure of his steps. Never off balance, always ready to react to a sudden move by the warriors around him.

Zaren looked at him, eyes narrowing and hand going to a blade at his side. Auric turned towards him, smiling a hard smile and spreading his empty hands. He said something in prytheen.

Around us, the warriors gasped.

20

AURIC

Clinging to the bottom of the flier on its trip back to the *Wandering Star* hadn't been easy, and I'd thought my arms would fall off by the time we descended. But it had gotten me inside and kept me close to my khara. That made it worth any amount of pain.

I had to take my time, clambering out from under the transport while all attention was on the confrontation. If he'd spotted me before I was ready to make my entrance, Zaren would have had me killed and the trip would have been useless. But once he struck Tamara, my anger took over. I had to intervene.

Tamara was unhurt, thank the blessed ones. Even so, I swore Zaren would pay for laying a hand on her. Keeping my rage on a tight leash, I walked towards my khara; losing control now wouldn't do her any good. Saving her would be hard enough if I did everything right, and the slightest mistake could kill us both.

Around me stood dozens of warriors who'd sworn to follow Zaren as their Alpha-Captain. Killers who had given up their honor in favor of riches and power, those who'd seen the need to follow him to survive, and those who simply came along for the ride. Some had been part of his clan before he'd turned from the Code, but that didn't excuse them. It was a warrior's responsibility to keep his Alpha honest, or to challenge him if he strayed too far from the path.

Others had even less excuse. Warriors from each of the seven clans of the Silver Band were here, even some who had once followed me. Now they obeyed Zaren in exchange for his protection and resources. A few even looked hopeful — counting on me to stand up to Zaren and fix things.

They might not like him or his leadership, but they weren't willing to stand up to him themselves. Cowards.

Forget them, focus on what matters. My khara is in danger. The warriors would help or they would not; either way, I had to stand up to Zaren and protect her.

"You dare show yourself here, traitor?" Zaren drew himself up, sheathing his claws and resting his hand on the grip of his pistol. The stolen human weapon looked out of place on his harness, but it was no less deadly for that.

Given half an excuse, he'd gun me down and call it an execution. To save my khara, I would have to tread carefully and put him in a position where simply killing me wasn't an option.

"I dare many things, more than you ever have," I said, pitching my voice to carry. "I dare to follow the Code of our ancestors, to use my strength to protect the weak rather than prey on them. To stand against injustice rather than perpetrate it. To put my honor before my life. You, Zaren, are unworthy of the title Alpha-Captain."

Around me, warriors shifted uncomfortably. Each of them had learned the Code while they were still kits, and no one wanted to think of themselves as dishonoring the legacy of the Band. It was all we had left of our homeworld.

Zaren looked around, measuring the crowd, and reluctantly took his hand off his pistol. Shooting me down would just prove my point. I wore armor made of honor, though it would only protect me so far.

"We are predators," he said. "Killers and hunters. The humans are prey animals, nothing more."

"No," I said, keeping my voice calm and even. It wasn't easy to keep my temper, but I had to. Showing my rage wouldn't help. "They are our equals, and I can prove it."

I stepped closer, moving slowly and carefully. Giving him no excuse to think I might attack him. Zaren watched me approach, his face carefully controlled. His calm didn't quite reach his eyes, though — they darted around, suspicious and angry, and I knew he wasn't comfortable.

Surrounded by his warriors, neither was I.

"We can mate-bond with the humans," I said, loud

enough to carry. "I have found my khara amongst them, and you cannot claim we can bond to inferiors."

Around us the warriors fell silent. All attention was on me now. Even the humans stared, though they didn't understand our words. It was clear we were discussing something important.

Zaren took a step forward, into arm's reach. Close enough that it would be hard for either of us to defend ourselves from a sudden attack by the other.

"You lie," he hissed. "They are just beasts, cowards and prey for us. No warrior's khara could be so low. Or perhaps, traitor, you are not a warrior at all?"

My jaw tightened and all my muscles strained to attack. By sheer effort of will I held myself back. It was easy to ignore the insult to me, but the insult to Tamara? I would have gutted him for it.

That was what he was hoping for. I saw it in his eyes. If I attacked, I would give him the pretext he needed to have me killed.

Perhaps I'd kill him, perhaps not, but one thing was certain — I wouldn't protect Tamara. She'd pay for my attack and that I would not allow.

"When you proposed this attack, you said we might find mates amongst the humans," I reminded him. "Are you saying that you lied?"

That stopped him for a moment, caught in a net of his own lies, but he rallied fast. "Of course not. But a female to mate with is different than a khara. We can take their females without them being our equals."

I thought my heart would explode with rage at

those words. The idea that he and his warriors would take females without considering them equals made me sick to my stomach, and I struggled to keep my anger from taking over. The next words he spoke were drowned out by the pounding of my furious pulse.

But the effect of his orders was clear. Prytheen warriors pulled humans from their workgroups, separating the females from the males. I saw tears and heard cries of pain from the humans, outbursts in their language. Soon one of them would snap. The humans were not the weaklings Zaren claimed they were. They would fight this, and they would die.

"Stop," I snapped. The cold, deadly fury in my voice made Zaren flinch back and his warriors froze.

"You betrayed your species and your clan," he answered. "I need not answer to you."

His hand went to his gun, and I readied myself to die fighting. Against these numbers there was no other outcome, even if the humans revolted at the same time. Better to die fighting than to allow this outrage, the final loss of the Silver Band's honor.

For a frozen moment we stood facing each other, each waiting for the other to make the first move. Before either of us did, though, Tamara intervened.

"Leave my khara alone!" She screamed the words, leaping at Zaren in a heroic, doomed display. Unarmed, she stood no chance.

There was nothing wrong with Zaren's reflexes. He stepped back out of my reach, turning and striking Tamara without taking his eyes off me. His blow turned her desperate leap into a painful tumble, straight into my path. Instinct took over and I abandoned my attack to catch her.

Zaren's pistol was in his hand before I could put her down. If he shot now it would tear through her on the way to me, and that I would not allow.

I stopped, turning away and putting my body between her and harm as I examined my khara. Rage flickered in her eyes but she was unhurt save for a bruise. That, at least, was good news.

I turned to glare at Zaren. "You struck my khara."

Around us, the warriors fell silent. It was a deadly accusation: to strike a warrior could be forgiven, but striking a warrior's khara could only end in death.

Zaren's eyes flicked around the camp, at his men. Too many were watching for him to simply murder me and ignore my words. He had to face my challenge.

"She is not prytheen," he said, loud, speaking more to the crowd than to me. "She has no protection under our laws, and you are a traitor."

I grinned, scenting weakness, and set Tamara down. Drawing myself up to my full height, I kept my attention on Zaren though I felt the weight of the crowd's attention on me. Humans and prytheen, all hanging on my words.

The fate of both species on this planet hung on what I did and said now.

"I found my khara amongst the humans," I said, speaking firmly. "You were right about that much, but no more. We are the Silver Band of Prytheen, warriors without peer, and the Code guides our steps. But a warrior is incomplete without his khara."

As much as I hated Zaren, I owed him a debt: without him, I would never have met my Tamara. Never have known that my khara was a human, and never known the happiness I'd found in her arms.

And never known the rage that burned in my heart when Zaren hurt her. I owed him a debt for that, too.

Caught on his own pretext for his dishonorable war, Zaren snarled wordlessly. I matched his snarl, letting my anger show as I spoke the words of challenge.

"Tamara-Engineer is my mate, my heart, my soul. She is *mine,* and you have hurt her. I will kill you for that as honor demands."

The surrounding warriors broke into murmurs, and I heard the news spreading through the camp. More and more prytheen gathered to watch our confrontation, and all of them knew the Code.

Some had even been my warriors before the attack. I couldn't count on them as allies, not after they'd accepted Zaren's authority, but I knew their temper. Zaren had to tread carefully if he wanted to dismiss my challenge.

"You are a fugitive, an oathbreaker," he blustered, looking around. I kept my eyes fixed on him, stalking forward. "Your word is worth nothing. I am alpha here, and my word is law."

I bared my fangs, feeling the crowd's attitude shift. No prytheen would accept a leader who wasn't a warrior, and he was starting to sound as though he wanted to avoid a fight.

That was exactly right, of course. He'd pulled himself to greatness by picking the easy battle, the least dangerous foe. A good way to win power, to gain riches with which to reward followers. And I wouldn't deny that he was a skilled leader — he knew how to make the most of his forces, and he'd managed to grind down the rest of the Silver Band.

But now, it was between him and me. And that was a fight he did not want.

Despite his fear, Zaren wasn't a coward. No one who allowed his fear to rule him could have made it to the top of the Band. Zaren wouldn't back down from a fight if it would cost him his authority.

"Very well," he said at last, looking around and weighing the mood of the crowd. "Tomorrow, then. At dawn, I will kill this traitor and mount his head on the wall as a warning. His treachery stranded us here, and I will avenge you all, my brothers."

His loyal warriors cheered, and I weighed the response in turn. Not every prytheen sounded enthusiastic, but he still had enough support that I couldn't count on the others to back me. And of course he would use me as a scapegoat. If he managed to lay the blame for the crash on me and win the duel, his position would be secure.

I have the duel I wanted, I reminded myself, blood pumping. *What he thinks will happen if he wins is of no consequence. I will kill him for hurting Tamara, and then we'll see who's loyal to his corpse.*

Tamara watched me without fear, and the calm confidence in her gaze touched me. She didn't understand what was happening any more than the other humans did, but that changed nothing. I felt her certainty that I would save her, and it calmed my rage and replaced it with a quieter strength. For her I would move mountains. One Codeless warrior? Not a problem.

Zaren stepped close again, too close for comfort, and the temptation to strike now was strong. I could have hurt him, perhaps slain him, before he had a chance to react. But honor bound me and he knew it. Until the duel, we were both safe from each other.

"So you love the human female," he whispered, quiet enough that only I would hear. "Thank you for confirming that we can mate with them, it strengthens my hand considerably. And thank you for showing me your weak point."

I fought down the urge to slit his throat. Tamara's calm strength buoyed me, and I refused to let Zaren bait me into a mistake. *If I attack now, then whether or not I kill him, my khara dies with me.*

Instead, I replied just as quietly. "You cannot threaten her. If any harm comes to her before the fight, everyone will know you for what you are."

His smile was anything but friendly. "You mistake me, Auric. I'm making you a promise. When you lose our duel, I will be merciful. Your human pet will live unharmed, in as much comfort as this blasted planet allows. I will see to it that all her needs are met."

I blinked, surprised and suspicious. That was far too reasonable for Zaren, the kind of offer an honorable warrior would make. From him, there had to be more. I stayed silent, waiting for him to show me the blade hidden by his courtesy.

Eyes narrowing, he whispered. "If you win, she will not be so lucky. I have enough loyal warriors to make sure she will not live to celebrate your victory. It will not be a pleasant death either, Auric. You may count on my warriors to hurt her as she dies."

My blood ran cold and I growled, letting my fury show. "I will slaughter you for threatening her."

"Perhaps," he said, a cold, cruel amusement in his voice. "But what will that win you? Her painful death in your arms? That is not a prize you will fight for, I think. Or you can throw the fight and make sure she has all the comfort I can show her."

"Why would I trust you?" I asked despite myself. I wanted to spit in his face, to kill him on the spot, but if I tried, I would certainly die — and worse, so would Tamara.

"Lying gains me nothing," he answered with a shrug. "Think about it: to me she's just one more slave. I can spare her and see to her comfort with no cost to myself. And while you may question my honor, you can't think I'd have risen this high if I made a habit of breaking my word."

He straightened, smirked, and stepped back. "Think on it. Tomorrow at dawn we will meet here."

With that, he turned his back. It would have been easy to kill him then and there, but instead I let him withdraw. No point in making myself look like a cowardly murderer. For all I knew, that was his plan — get me to try and kill him, and one of his warriors would gun me down. That would be an end to it.

I refused to make things easy for him, and in two steps he was out of my reach.

That left me alone in the middle of the *Wandering Star's* deck. The humans were herded back to work and no prytheen wanted anything to do with me. Even those who agreed with me stayed back, and I didn't blame them. If Zaren won our fight the next day, none of my friends would last long under his rule.

21

TAMARA

My jaw ached where Zaren had hit me, but that was the least of my worries. Around me, the gathered prytheen watched Auric and Zaren as they talked in tones too low to overhear.

Whatever they were saying, it didn't leave Auric happy. I saw the anger and frustration in his tense muscles, and it boiled over into me.

One of the prytheen grabbed at my arm as they started pushing the other humans back to work. I shrugged him off, darting to Auric's side before the alien reacted. That might get me in trouble, but I had to know what was going on.

Auric fixed the other prytheen with a glare that froze him in place and snarled something. I caught the word 'khara' and no more, but whatever he said, it made the warrior back away. For a moment, at least, we had space to ourselves on the deck.

"What the hell's happening?" I demanded, my fear

turning into anger as I spoke. The pain in Auric's eyes sent a wave of guilt through me.

"I am sorry, my khara," he said, his hand resting on my shoulder and squeezing gently. "I tried to free you, but I fear I have only made things worse."

I took his wrist in my hands, holding on and trying to calm the panic that flared in me at his words. Forming a question wasn't easy — I tried to speak, but no words came.

Auric's hand tightened on my shoulder, and we drew strength from each other. His smile wasn't convincing, but it calmed me enough that I could listen.

"We have little time," he said, voice quiet and fast. "My beloved, I challenged Zaren to a fight for you. We will face each other tomorrow morning in a battle to the death."

I swallowed, terror and hope both blossoming in my mind. "You'll win, right? You'll kill him and then this will be over?"

"I can promise nothing," he said. The darkness in his heart made me shiver, and I looked into his eyes.

Auric wouldn't lie to me. But that didn't mean that he wouldn't hide things from me, and I put two and two together.

Hoping I'd come up with five, I asked: "Are you going to *try* to win?"

He winced and my heart fell. For once I hated being right, but I understood how a bully's mind worked. I'd met plenty of them on Earth. "He's threatening me, isn't he? If you give him a real fight, he'll kill me."

"I will not allow anyone to harm you," Auric said, ducking the question. That was enough for me to fill in the gaps. "Tamara, you are my mate, my soul. I cannot allow you to be in danger."

"How do you think I feel?" I said, my hands gripping his wrist tight, tears welling in my eyes. "If you win, you can at least save my people. I'd rather that than watch you die and live to see them in slavery."

I tried to be brave, to ignore my fear for my own safety. It wasn't easy, not with the prytheen hunters prowling around us. If they wanted me dead, there wasn't anything I'd be able to do to stop it. I was at their mercy.

"Tamara, my love, I cannot do something that I know will kill you," Auric said. His voice was rough, full of pain, and his eyes glittered with tears. This tested even his immense strength. "I would do anything for your safety."

"God damn it, Auric, please. Win this fight." I couldn't stop the tears now, my vision blurring and my breathing coming quickly.

Strong hands closed on my arms as the prytheen came to drag me away. For a moment I considered fighting — what was the worst that could happen? If they killed me, they'd lose their hold over Auric.

But if I fought now, Auric would try to protect me. And he'd lose. Outnumbered as we were, we didn't stand a chance in hell.

As tempting as dying by his side was, I wouldn't start a fight that would end in Auric's death. Facing that thought made me understand how he felt, and tears rolled down my cheeks as I let the guards drag me away from him.

∼

THE CELL they dragged me to didn't really live up to the name. It had been a cargo container once, before the wall tore off during the crash and whatever had been inside had scattered across the landscape outside. I hoped it wasn't anything too vital, because I doubted we'd be able to salvage it.

But the container made a handy place for the prytheen to keep their captives. I sat against the metal wall, looking at the hastily-patched tear and thinking about how to seal it against vacuum again. A pointless problem, but better than worrying about what would happen in the morning.

Around me sat other humans, all dressed in the jumpsuits of the Arcadia Colony. Colonists I was supposed to be ferrying to their new home, awakened into this nightmare of slavery. I swallowed, unable to make eye contact. It wasn't my fault they were here, but I still felt responsible.

The other prisoners looked at me sullenly, hope lost, and then went back to their quiet conversations. No one wanted to be too close, which hurt. I understood — who'd want to invite the anger of their alien masters by being my friend? But it didn't make me feel any better.

There was one person I knew amongst the crowd of strangers. Dr. Orson made her way over and sat beside me, her gaze falling on the marks the tenger's sting had left on my forearm. She frowned. "What have you gotten yourself into, Captain?"

I blinked, taken by surprise and not knowing what to say. "What the hell, Doc?"

She shrugged, grabbing my arm unceremoniously and poked at the marks. Wincing, I pulled my arm away as she spoke.

"It's either you or me, and I'm too busy being a damned doctor," she said. "The aliens shot Donovan, McKenzie didn't make it through the crash, and I haven't seen Maxwell since planetfall. That leaves you."

I swallowed, taking back some of the things I'd thought about McKenzie. Sure, he'd been a creep of a man, but he'd died getting the ship down half-way intact which had to count for something. *Braver than I thought, anyway.*

But damn him for dying and leaving me in as ranking officer. Orson was right, though, it was down to her or me. Great. Now I had to take responsibility for this mess, too.

"I can't be in charge," I protested. "This was my first flight. I don't have any training—"

"Yeah, well, how much training do you think Donovan had for *this?*" Orson said, talking over me and fishing something from her medkit. "Look, someone has to be in charge. I need to focus on the injured. You're an officer. Done."

An icy spray on my wrist numbed me and I saw the dark marks fade a little. Orson nodded. "Anti-toxin works fine then. Good. You're lucky you got a low dose of the venom, it's pretty nasty. Saw a few colonists with it before the prytheen let us put up the forcefield to keep the animals at bay."

"You've got to wonder what they hunt for them to need venom like that," I said, shaking my head. I'd learned to ignore the stinging itch in my arm but now it was gone I felt a lot better. "At least they're keeping us safe from the animals."

Orson snorted, an undignified sound. "Sure. They don't want anyone else killing us, not when we're their farm workers."

One of the nearby colonists looked up from the holobook she was reading and shook her head.

"Some of them aren't so bad," she said. "One saved my life, remember."

"They don't want to waste workers, Dallas," Orson snapped. "That's not kindness, that's just being a smart slaver. I didn't say they were *stupid*."

"No," Dallas insisted. "No, he saved me from another of the aliens. They're not all comfortable with keeping slaves. You can see it in their eyes sometimes."

"Wishful thinking. Stockholm syndrome." Orson shook her head. "Dallas, you're seeing what you want to see."

"No," I said, letting an idea form as I spoke. "No, I

think she's right. Auric doesn't want to keep slaves, and he can't be the only one. If Auric can take control of the prytheen, we'll be able to live in peace."

Orson gave me a *look* and I shrugged. Maybe she was right, maybe I was seeing what I wanted to see. It didn't matter. Either I was right or we didn't stand a chance. There were too many of the prytheen and they were too dangerous — getting rid of all of them would be impossible.

Great, now I'm actually thinking about that. I sighed. There was no putting it off, someone had to make a plan. I couldn't just hope that Auric found a way out of the trap Zaren had caught him in.

Thinking about him sent a painful pang through my heart and I took a deep, shuddering breath. The pain in Auric's eyes when he looked at me, the certainty that he would die, ate at me.

How could you let yourself get trapped like this? I wanted to scream at him, but I wouldn't even get a chance to do that. If I spoke to him before his fight, I couldn't burden him with my pain.

I closed my eyes, a tear running down my cheek as I tried to get my imagination under control. It was hard to keep myself from visualizing Auric lying dead.

This was all my fault. If not for me, he'd have a fighting chance. But he couldn't bear to win if it meant my death, I knew. No more than I'd be able to watch him die if I had a way to stop it.

Which just means you have to find a way out, I told myself firmly, pushing down that pain and fear. Auric could win the fight, I was sure of it. I just needed to give him a chance to do it.

Opening my eyes, I dragged a sleeve across my face and dried my tears. They wouldn't help anyone.

I'm an engineer, I told myself. *I solve problems. That's what I do.*

Maybe if I approached this as an engineering problem to be solved, I could stop thinking about it as a death sentence for the man I loved. There *had* to be a way out.

Dr. Orson whispered into her wristband, dictating notes to the animated paperclip that was her interface. I looked around. Dallas was reading a holobook from hers. The rest of the colonists all wore their wristbands too. They'd been a fixture of life aboard the *Wandering Star* for so long that I hadn't really noticed them until now.

"Why did they leave us our communicators?" I asked Dallas. They didn't have much value as weapons but Zaren didn't strike me as someone who'd leave his slaves any tools that might help a rebellion.

"Most of us suck at Galtrade," Dallas answered, shaking her head. "The hologram translator isn't much, but it's better than nothing — and the aliens need us to understand orders. Not that they're very forgiving when that doesn't work out."

She sounded bitter, and I shivered at the idea of being reliant on Mr. Mews' translation skills to avoid a beating. But it meant that we had our wristbands, and that might be useful.

"Dallas, was it?" I asked. The colonist nodded, smiling just a little.

"Hayley Dallas, but everyone just calls me Dallas," she said. "Colony communications tech. If we ever get to Arcadia, that is."

"We'll do our best to get you there," I promised. "I'm Tamara."

I couldn't introduce myself as captain. That would need a while to sink in, even if I accepted the logic.

"Every human's got their comm?" I asked, wanting to be sure. The seed of an idea was forming, and I turned it over in my mind as Dallas answered.

"That's right, Captain." She nodded emphatically and I winced at the title. *Guess I'll have to get used to it.* "The aliens won't lower themselves to learn our language, and they don't have the time to teach us theirs. Our holograms can translate and help us learn, so we get to keep them."

It was a safe enough move on their part. The prytheen had nothing to fear from the communicators, not with the way they were locked down for safety. Everything ran through the *Wandering Star's* systems, so as long as the prytheen controlled the ship we'd have no privacy. They'd be able to monitor any conversations we had over them. Maybe not *understand* them, given the language barrier, but if they were willing to simply punish anyone who used them, that didn't matter.

Without authority over the *Wandering Star's* computer systems, the colonists couldn't do anything about that. But I had a few tricks up my sleeve that they didn't, and authority the ship's systems might recognize. I tried not to let myself hope too much.

"The local animals, have they been much trouble?" I asked. "The things out in the woods were pretty dangerous."

Dr. Orson shrugged. "There are plenty of nasties out there. Lots of toxic predators, for a start, and they seem to be drawn to the crash. We're lucky that the forcefield holds them back."

"Yeah," Dallas chimed in. "One of those snake-bird things killed a prytheen before they worked out that they were venomous. That's why they switched on the field, I think. That and it makes it easy to spot anyone coming in or out."

I wondered who that prytheen warrior had been. From the satisfied note in her voice when she spoke of his death, I suspected there was some history there. It didn't seem like something to pry into, though.

Doesn't matter anyway. For now, what matters is that there are dangerous animals nearby.

"You're a comms tech. Does that mean you can get the communicators to do what you want?" I asked Dallas. She frowned as I continued. "I need to get a message out to everyone. Can you do that?"

"I *can*," she said cautiously. "That's not hard, especially for the captain. But the aliens listen in to everything."

"Sure." I nodded, leaning close. "That just means you have to be smarter than whoever they've got running their listening program, right? You can outsmart some alien who doesn't know the system."

"If they hear—" she cut off, shook her head. Drew a breath and pulled herself together. "It would have to be a recording. I can ping that to everyone's comm, have the hologram play it as an update from the captain. No way to get a reply back, though, not without them noticing."

She looked unhappy, checking her wristband. A hologram of a puppy appeared, looking back at her and panting. "The system's limited by design. Pushing it outside its comfort zone won't be easy, and I can't promise it will work."

"That's fine," I assured her, hoping it really would be. I'd only get one chance at this, and if it didn't work, I'd make things worse for everyone. No point in worrying, though. "Just do your best, it's all we can do. Get it set up, and I'll work out what I want to send. There'll need to be two recordings, though."

Dr. Orson looked at us and frowned. "Is this a good idea?"

No, I thought. *It's a terrible idea and might get all of us killed.* I couldn't say that, though. If we didn't try this, we might not get another chance. We *definitely* wouldn't get one before Auric died. "Yes. I know what I'm doing, and we only get one shot at this. Don't worry, Doc. I've got a plan."

22

AURIC

I marched out onto the deck as the sun rose over the horizon. In the distance, some strange creature sang to greet the dawn, a strange alien trilling that echoed from every direction. Whatever the alien was, the *Wandering Star's* forcefield kept them from coming too close to the colony ship. Given my experience with the planet's wildlife, that was for the best.

The human colonists were already gathered around the edge of the deck, there to see the death of their would-be savior. To see what happened when someone challenged the alpha of the Silver Band. Zaren would not waste the chance to intimidate his new slaves.

Prytheen warriors stood around the humans, watching them. One of those guards would be the executioner waiting to strike down Tamara if I didn't play my part. I tried not to think about that.

Near the center of the black metal deck a circle of prytheen warriors waited for me. Those were the real audience for this, the warriors who'd joined Zaren. The ones he needed to impress, and to whom he needed to prove his dominance.

And there was Zaren, the picture of confidence. His eyes gleamed and a smile tugged at his lips as he watched me approach. There was no sign of doubt about him, no clue that he didn't believe in his ability to kill me.

I stopped just out of reach of him. More humans were filing out of the ship, Tamara amongst them. One of the guards watched her carefully, his hand on the hilt of a knife. Of course Zaren wanted to make sure I saw Tamara and her executioner. He needed me to remember his threat.

Not that I would forget it for a second. Through the dark hours of the night it had been all I could think about, keeping me from sleep. My mind had chased down every possible outcome, to no avail.

I knew that I would do anything to spare her life. If that meant my death, so be it. Her life mattered more to me than my own, more than anything.

I met Zaren's eyes and nodded, just a fraction. His smile broadened.

"You have challenged me, traitor," he said, spreading his arms wide and speaking loudly for all to hear. "And now I will kill you for the harm you have done the Silver Band. Let everyone see who leads here, who is Alpha-of-Alphas."

A murmur ran through the crowd as he claimed that title for himself, and I wondered what the other alphas would say when they heard of it. None of them were here, and I didn't know whether they were even on the planet.

Zaren was claiming a legendary title that no one had held since the founding of the Silver Band. Sole rulership over every warrior, mastery even of the other alphas — a few had tried to claim that place over the centuries but none had survived to use the title.

I almost admired Zaren's gall in using this disaster to take that position. Almost.

"There has only ever been one Alpha-of-Alphas," I said, unable to let that pass. "You are no fit heir to the title, Zaren. Or do you think you are Printhar reborn?"

He laughed, shrugging off my objection. "If we are to live, we must have unity. And that means we need a single voice to lead us, as Printhar did when he forged the Silver Band. *My* voice, Auric, mine alone, can restore us to the stars."

A few of his loyalists cheered that, and the other prytheen joined in. No one wanted to make an enemy of their alpha, not here and now. *Cowards,* I thought, glaring around.

But that wasn't fair, not to all of them. Starting a civil war would doom everyone, given how few resources we had to spare. The warriors were trapped as long as Zaren had loyalists to fight for him.

My challenge was their way out — and if I won, they would follow me as they followed Zaren now.

Unfortunately for us all, Zaren had taken steps to control that possibility.

Tamara. My eyes flicked up to her, one last look at my khara before the fight began. She stood stiff, her emotions locked down under a tight control that didn't fool me for a moment. The fear she refused to show leaked out into my soul as our eyes met.

Do not worry, I tried to tell her. *You will be safe. No matter what, I will protect you.*

It wasn't easy to believe, even for me. And I had no time to reassure her properly. The fight was about to begin.

The oldest warrior present, Kardan, stepped forward to judge. He looked from one of us to the other, unhappy with his place in this but unwilling to step away from the position tradition gave him in a fight between alphas.

"Fight with honor," he said. "Remember our ancestors, and the Code they passed down to us. This fight will be settled only by the death of an alpha."

His ritual words hung in the air between us for a moment, and the audience watched in hushed silence. Kardan stepped back and raised a hand.

"Begin!"

~

I MOVED FIRST, as soon as Kardan gave the word. My pounce carried me at Zaren, nearly bowling him over before he had a chance to react.

He'd not expected me to take the initiative, and that gave me a moment's advantage. But he was skilled too, and fast, and uninjured. My strikes glanced off his blocks as he scrambled back, and then he ducked to the side, disengaging.

My hands flexed, claws extending, and I wished that I'd managed more than glancing blows. However this ended, I wanted to make sure he remembered this fight forever.

A nice set of scars across the face would do, even if I couldn't open his throat.

As we circled each other, the humans cheered and a few prytheen warriors joined them. At least I had some supporters here — and from the expression on his face, Zaren didn't like that.

Tough. If you want our people to love you, you need to do something more than lead them on a disastrous raid. I didn't say it out loud, but I didn't have to. Zaren's angry glare told me he knew what I was thinking.

"We'll see how much they cheer when I open your belly and feed your guts to the birds," he snarled, baring his fangs. His eyes flicked from me to Tamara, a reminder of what was at stake if I didn't give in.

Fury welled up inside me, a towering inferno of emotion I couldn't control. Before I knew what I was doing, I was attacking again, driving him back. This time, though, he was prepared — and my frenzied attacks left me open to his counter.

A blazing pain across my chest followed his raking claws, and I only just avoided a lethal cut to my throat.

In return I opened a cut on his shoulder before I dodged away.

Zaren followed, pressing his advantage, and I didn't dare try to take the openings he gave me. Not when it would mean Tamara's painful death. Zaren's claws sliced past my face, a narrow miss that would have blinded me, and my counter sliced into his ear.

He hissed in pain, kicking at my leg in an attempt at a trip. I could have caught him then, grabbed his foot and opened the artery in his thigh. Instinct almost brought my hand down before I stopped myself, and I barely managed to fumble the attack.

If I'd connected, Zaren would have bled out in seconds.

Around us, the circle of warriors hissed as I nearly won, and Zaren's eyes flashed with the burning fury of humiliation. His attacks got quicker, more ferocious and sloppier.

If I'd been willing to take advantage of the openings he gave me, I'd have killed him a dozen times in as many seconds. Instead, I fell back, raising my right arm to fend off Zaren's claws. He tore bloody gouges through my flesh, and burning pain shot through me as I struggled to keep my arm up.

Zaren saw his chance and pressed forward, opening more cuts on my injured arm as I backpedaled, barely avoiding a deadly attack.

My eyes flicked up to the audience. Amongst the humans, Tamara watched, a look of horror on her face.

I'm sorry, my love, I thought. The watching warrior behind her reinforced the danger she was in, and as long as he threatened her, I had no choice. I couldn't allow myself to win this fight.

23

TAMARA

I watched Auric and Zaren circle each other, both bloodied and battered from their exchange. The crowd roared, but the pounding of my heart drowned out the noise. Blood trailed down Auric's wounded arms, his graceful movements were faltering, and I knew that he wouldn't last long. His right arm hung at his side, but he kept his left up, defending himself as best he could one-handed.

Zaren didn't look much better, but the nasty grin spreading across his face showed his confidence. The cuts to his chest looked deep, painful, but they wouldn't stop him. Whoever won that fight would come away with scars that would mark them for life.

It had to be Auric. He had to win. I couldn't survive without him. Even if it meant my death — and the irony of that wasn't lost on me. We would each rather die than see the other suffer.

One of Zaren's warriors stood behind me, his eyes

boring into my back. I felt the danger, though I knew he didn't care about me. The threat was meant for Auric, and he'd be bound by it. But I wouldn't. If I was going to act, it had to be now.

To my surprise, my fingers were steady as I brushed my wristband. The other humans crowding around me watching the duel gave me cover, and I glanced down to see Mr. Mews flicker into existence. Not the best interface to manage hacking through, but I had to work with what I had. Though the ship's systems accepted my authority, I was still trying to ask them to do something they were programmed not to.

Dallas had suggested doing this part during the night, and it would certainly have been easier in the cell. But it would also have been too easy for the prytheen on the bridge to notice me accessing the engineering systems remotely. Now that the fight had started, I hoped they were watching like everyone else. I only needed a few minutes' distraction.

I worked quickly, trying to focus on the work without being obvious. It wasn't easy, but the fight kept the eyes of most of the aliens off me as I muttered commands to Mr. Mews and muted his protests. The hardest part was focusing on the work and not on my lover's desperate fight.

In the circle, Zaren darted forward, his clawed hand slashing past Auric's face. My mate ducked back just in time, rolling to the side as Zaren pursued him, and I gasped as blood sprayed. Another shallow cut, not fatal but dangerous. I was running out of time.

Mr. Mews yowled a warning as I overrode the safeties, and I cursed. The alien warrior watching me must have heard that. I glanced round and sure enough, he was frowning and pushing through the crowd towards me. There was no time to check my work now, I'd just have to trust I'd done it right.

"Do it," I told Mr. Mews, sending the command to the *Wandering Star's* computers and praying I'd set them up right.

At the edge of the camp the forcefield whined audibly and failed with a bang that echoed across the deck of the *Wandering Star*. The planet's wildlife rushed to the attack.

For a moment, none of the prytheen moved. The terrifying howls of the charging predators shocked them into immobility. Auric was the only one not affected, bounding forward to slam into Zaren with all his weight, smashing the two of them to the deck in a heap.

Before the rest of them had a chance to react, the humans surged forward. Alone, not one of us was a match for even the weakest prytheen warrior. As a mass, though, we rolled over several of them before they had a chance to react.

Every colonist's wristband hummed, reproducing the sounds that drove the predators wild at full volume. All morning we'd been driving the animals outside the forcefield crazy and now they could get in they were charging for the source of the maddening noise.

In seconds we'd be at the center of a wave of furious wildlife, and we had to take advantage of the moment or we'd all die. My plan was, I admitted, crazy. But this wasn't the time to doubt it.

I tore my wristband off, wished Mr. Mews well, and threw it as hard as I could at the prytheen charging towards me.

There was nothing wrong with his reflexes. He snatched the wristband out of the air without slowing, his other hand pulling a knife. I saw my death in his eyes.

And then a tenger pounced on him, stingers wrapping around his arm, claws tearing. With a blood-curdling scream, my would-be executioner fell under the creature's assault.

All around me, humans threw their wristbands at the aliens and scattered. We'd known what was coming, the prytheen didn't, and by the time they figured it out, everything was in chaos. When one prytheen made it into the crowd, he was torn apart by a mass of humans.

They went down fighting, knives flashing and claws tearing. But they went down.

"No!" Zaren cried out, one of the few prytheen words I'd picked up. He turned and ran for the bridge, not fleeing but trying to take command of his forces in the chaos. If he rallied them, he'd win.

Auric stepped into his path, standing between him and his goal. No longer tentative, restrained. My khara stood tall, ignoring his wounds and snarling a challenge.

The fight for the Silver Band had begun in earnest.

I tried to focus on my own situation but it was impossible. My beloved moved with a grace I couldn't look away from, blurring into an attack that sent Zaren flying. Each stroke of Auric's claws slashed close to his enemy, but Zaren was so *fast*. Fast enough to stay out of the way, to dodge back and roll and scramble aside.

Someone jostled me and I found myself carried along by the crowd of humans fleeing the deck. Around us, animals roared and hooted, ripping into the prytheen as they tried to rally. The aliens were warriors, trained and skilled, and it wouldn't be long before they got the deck under control. The chaos would only give us the upper hand for seconds and we had to make the most of it.

Fleeing through the airlocks into the *Wandering Star* put strong steel walls between us and the aliens, and as soon as everyone was inside, I hit the emergency override. The airlock doors slammed shut, locking the prytheen outside with the outraged animals.

We didn't stop. Once the prytheen rallied, those doors wouldn't hold them for long and we needed control of the ship if our rebellion was going to mean anything. I turned, rushing for the bridge behind with the other colonists, a headlong dash to take control of the systems which were still working.

By the time I arrived, the bridge was under human control and a lone prytheen warrior sat glowering at his captors. The fight had been quick and brutal — one human lay dead, one clutched at his wounded leg, but another held a heavy pistol leveled at the alien.

I ignored them, desperate to see how the fight outside was going.

The armored glass window let me look down at the deck through a smear of prytheen blood. The crack of gunfire filled the air, but the animals didn't care about casualties — crazed by ultrasound, they rushed headlong into danger.

I spared the ongoing battle only a moment's glance though. Beyond it, in a space still clear of animals, Zaren and Auric fought like demons.

Both were streaked with blood, wounds deep on their skin, but neither seemed willing to give up. Surrender meant death, after all — there could be no prisoners when two alphas fought. I watched, heart in my throat, as Auric tumbled back with a fresh cut across his chest. Zaren followed slowly, catching his breath.

They snarled at each other, pure rage in their voices. No words: the time for speech had passed, and neither had anything left to say to the other.

Auric's right arm hung limp at his side, blood dripping down it from deep gashes. His left, though, slashed fast enough to drive Zaren back. But for how long? Could he win with only one arm? My hands pressed to the cool glass and I muttered a prayer under my breath. He *had* to win. Never mind what Zaren would do to me and the other humans: I couldn't face watching Auric die.

Damn you Auric, win. You have to win.

Maybe he heard my thoughts, maybe it was something else that drew his eye to me, but Auric looked up. His gaze met mine across the bloody deck and I saw calm acceptance in him. Whatever happened here, he loved me and I loved him and that would be enough.

Not for me, I thought. He couldn't really hear me, I knew, but I had to try. *I need you to live Auric. I need you.*

Zaren spotted Auric's distraction and pounced, putting all of his weight behind a powerful attack that slammed Auric to the deck. I gasped, hammering on the glass, as my lover's enemy tore into his good arm, knocking it aside. Pinning Auric to the floor beneath him.

Auric slashed with his left hand, claws gleaming red. Zaren just laughed, catching Auric's wrist in one hand and forcing the arm down.

I stared as he pinned Auric's good arm down with both of his, leaning over my beloved. Teeth bared, he angled himself to bite out Auric's throat. I couldn't look away. It was awful, terrible, and I wanted to hide. To cover my eyes. Anything but watch this awful sight.

But I couldn't, I was frozen in place. Everything seemed to be moving in slow motion as Zaren lowered his mouth towards Auric's neck.

And then Auric's right arm came up. Despite the injuries, the blood, it moved with speed and grace and above all *force*, and Zaren froze as Auric slashed across his throat.

My eyes were as wide as Zaren's. Auric had faked his injury — for the whole fight he'd let that arm hang limp, let Zaren attack him, all to set up this one surprise attack. He'd nearly *died* setting it up.

It had been worth it. Zaren reared back, but he was a moment too slow. Auric's claws dug deep, a shower of blood sprayed across the deck, and then Zaren pulled away. Auric jumped to his feet as Zaren fell, blood pumping from his torn throat.

Bloodied, battered, injured, but *alive,* Auric stood tall. Raising his bloody hands high, Auric roared, a sound that shook me even through the glass. Outside, every prytheen warrior looked to him, even those engaged in their own life or death struggles.

"I am ALPHA," Auric shouted, and my heart beat again. After what felt like years, I could move and breathe and speak.

"Kill the ultrasound," I called over my shoulder. Dallas had been waiting for my order at the communications console. She hit a button and the ultrasonic howl that enraged the wildlife cut off, a strange pressure vanishing from the air. Below me I saw the animals panic. Without the ultrasound to enrage them, none of the predators wanted to stay in the losing fight. In seconds the decks were clear of predators, leaving the bloodied prytheen to look on in wonder.

We'd won. I could hardly believe it, but we'd *won.*

24

AURIC

All around me, the warriors of the Silver Band stared. Some were injured, some dead, all shaken. None of them seemed certain of what to do.

But I stood over the gasping, dying form of their leader. My victory was clear, indisputable. I glared at the first warrior to raise a weapon my way, meeting his gaze steadily until he lowered the gun.

"I am alpha," I repeated, quieter this time but no less firmly. "I claim my victory by the Code. Does anyone dispute it?"

A few grumbled, which wasn't a good sign for the future. But no one argued the point. Which was good — I could stand tall and threaten, but I doubted I could win another fight in my condition.

"Give me your gun," I ordered the nearest warrior. He complied without question, and I hid the wince as I held it in my wounded hand.

I'd been faking the extent of my injury, but my right arm was still badly hurt. This was no time to show weakness, though.

"Now we make peace with the humans," I said, loud enough for my voice to carry. "No harm is to come to them."

"They killed half of us," one of my new followers hissed. "We cannot have peace until they have paid for that crime."

"They defended themselves," I snapped. There was no time for this foolishness. "You attacked them, tried to enslave them. They found a clever way to fight back and throw you off — would you have done differently if you were in their place?"

Dafram, I think his name is. I looked the young warrior in the eye until he dropped his gaze and shuffled, embarrassed. *Good. Perhaps they can be saved.*

Killing Zaren had been the easy part. Undoing the damage he'd done to the Silver Band would be the work of a lifetime, perhaps more, but there was a heart of honor beating inside every prytheen. Bringing it out would be hard work, but it could be done.

And I'd never shied away from hard work.

"The humans have shown themselves our equals today," I announced. "We will treat with them honorably, and together perhaps we can return to the stars. If we fight them, then even in victory we would gain nothing."

Dafram nodded, and around me the rest of the

Band started to mutter agreement. I took note of who was most reluctant. This would be a hard transition for many, and I had to pay attention to who might cause trouble, but for today I had them on my side.

Not least because so many needed medical treatment after the animal attack.

Turning to the bridge that towered over the deck, I looked up. There was Tamara, my khara, my beloved. She looked down at me, uninjured, and the last of my fears evaporated. Her plan had worked. She was alive, and as far as I could see, unhurt.

We'd won.

"Open the doors," I said, switching to Galtrade for the benefit of the humans.

Tamara looked at me, her face pale, the glass between us stained with prytheen blood. Her fingers drummed nervously on the glass.

"No," she replied, speakers amplifying her voice. I blinked. That was not the response I'd expected from my beloved.

"We humans hold the *Wandering Star* again," she continued after a moment, nerves giving way to steel. "And I am the highest-ranking officer left. That makes me the captain of this ship, and if you're serious about respecting me, respecting *us*, then you don't give me orders."

Around me, the warriors of the Silver Band straightened. Readied their weapons. Their alpha was being challenged, and that drew them together behind me just as they'd backed Zaren before. Weapons hummed as they were dialed up to maximum charge, enough to shatter that armored glass and expose the bridge.

I raised a hand, signaling *no.* Tamara was right — this was not our ship. It belonged to the humans, and my khara was their leader.

That would take some getting used to. My instincts told me that she was *mine*, and to tear down any obstacle in my way. But if the humans were our equals, that held true for the two of us as well.

"In that case, Captain," I said carefully, "permission to come aboard?"

Tamara's grin lit up her face and I felt my spirits buoyed by the sight of her joy. She gestured behind her and the doors hissed open as her crew obeyed her command.

"Welcome aboard, Alpha," she said.

∽

ALL OF US, humans and prytheen, felt the tension hanging in the air but no one wanted another fight. Moving through the *Wandering Star*, I felt the eyes of the humans watching from the doorways I passed. Men and women stared at me, and I felt a familiar itch between my shoulder blades.

The human colonists watched warily as I approached their captain, but Tamara stepped forward without fear. She extended her hand in a human greeting that I ignored, sweeping her up in my arms and hugging her tight.

"We *won*, khara," I said. She gasped for air, grinned, and kissed me.

"We did," she agreed. Looking around at the eyes on us, she blushed and squirmed out of my grip. "Now comes the tricky bit. What do we do with our victory?"

I opened my mouth, then closed it again. The tricky bit indeed. No matter where we went from here, though, there were some things that needed to be taken care of. We could start with those. "First, we tend the injured. Both sides took casualties in the fighting, and too many have died already."

That got nods from everyone who understood, some humans whispering translations for the rest. We would have to do something about that language barrier, I realized, filing the thought for later. There were a lot of things we'd need to take care of, and it was dizzying to think of the responsibility that we were taking on.

"Dr. Orson is in the sickbay, setting up," Tamara said. The tension in her voice told me she was having the same realization. "We'll treat your injured as best we can, but I don't know if we have the supplies you'll need."

"We'll make do," I assured her. "Some of my people are medics, they will help."

There would be arguments, of course, but they

would help the doctor. I was in no mood to put up with complaints and with Zaren's corpse still cooling I doubted that anyone would push the issue. For a little while, at least, I could count on cooperation even from Zaren's loyalists.

I envied Tamara. The humans looked at her with awe; she would have no difficulty getting her people to obey.

"Then we need to reach out to everyone else who's crashed here," Tamara continued. "Make sure that the prytheen know Zaren's not in charge anymore, and the humans know you aren't all the enemy."

I nodded, frowning. Zaren hadn't been the sole ruler of the Band, and there was no guarantee that every prytheen on the planet would acknowledge me as alpha. I didn't even know if there were other alphas on the planet — if there were, then I'd be one leader amongst several. Still, anything we could do to stop more fighting would be worthwhile.

"There are many details to work out," I said. "We should start with the simplest. I propose an alliance between our people: humans and prytheen, working together."

"I won't put my people under your command," Tamara said. "I'm sorry, Auric, but we can't trust the prytheen."

That hurt, but I couldn't argue. The warriors following me had abandoned the Code once — it would be foolish of Tamara to ignore the possibility that they'd do it again. That *we'd* do it again.

"My warriors will not obey you," I replied. "The Silver Band is prytheen and I cannot put them at the service of another species."

She nodded. Smiled. "So we share command. You rule the prytheen, I command the humans, and we sort out a government that suits everyone."

"That will take some doing," I pointed out.

"Oh no," Tamara replied, eyes gleaming as she grinned. "Lots of meetings, just the two of us, working late into the night. However will we cope?"

I couldn't contain my laugh and reached for her again. Tamara stepped back, putting a hand to my chest and holding me off.

"Not so fast," she said. "You're hurt. Go get yourself checked out and then you can hug me."

I wanted to protest, but I could see my blood on her hands. Zaren's claws had bitten deep and the pain was starting to catch up. Tamara was right. I needed medical attention.

But I didn't let that stop me. Grabbing Tamara, I lifted her up and kissed her hard on the lips, silencing her squeal of surprised protest as we spun around the bridge. A ragged cheer went up from both the prytheen and humans gathered around us, but we paid them no heed. My full attention was on her, the feel of her lips against mine, the taste of her, the delightful feeling of her body pressed to mine.

Tamara melted against me, her protests forgotten in the whirlwind of emotion that gripped us both. By the time I set her down we were both breathless and I could feel her joy through the khara-bond that linked us. She tried to frown but couldn't hide her smile as she swatted me on my good arm.

"*Now* I will go see your doctor," I told her, turning and walking off the bridge with a spring in my step.

25

TAMARA

"I can't work in these conditions," Dr. Orson complained when I came to look in on her a week later. The same complaint she'd made every day since the rebellion, but it wasn't a joke. Patients spilled out into the corridors around sickbay, and she had no qualified help. Orson worked constantly, and as far as I knew, our little meetings were the only breaks she took.

"If we find any nurses, I'll send them to you straight away," I promised for the twentieth time. "But it looks like you're doing a great job under the circumstances, Doc."

She snorted and shook her head, but there was a spark in her eyes. A hint that she was pleased with how things were going. And the room looked a little less full than it had the day before. Since no one had reported any deaths that was a good sign.

"It helps that the prytheen don't need much," she

said, pushing a hand through her messy hair. "Patch up the worst of their injuries and they go into a trance. I wish *humans* were that convenient. What about your work?"

I failed to hold back a groan. "Which bit, engineer or captain? Neither's great. I've finally finished the inventory of damage to the *Wandering Star*, and..."

Orson pulled a face. "And we're not going anywhere."

"Yeah. The hyperdrive might be repairable, but the thrusters are finished. No way I can get them fixed without a full space dock, and spare parts we can't build here." I leaned against the wall resisting the urge to put my head in my hands. "Plus, the hull damage is bad. We *might* be able to repair it, but there are other things we can use those resources for."

Dr. Orson snorted. "I didn't expect to get off world any time soon. I'm just glad you're the one stuck running the colony, not me."

That made me grimace. The endless meetings would only get worse if we were stuck here, but we had so many decisions to make. What work was essential, what could we put off? Did we need a police force, an army? Where were we going to plant farms, who would run the power plant?

I'd hoped that we wouldn't need to make those choices — if the *Wandering Star* could take us home, we wouldn't need them. But if we were trapped on this planet...

"We can't even get everyone here," I complained.

"Half the colonists are scattered around the planet with broken colony pods."

"And your boyfriend's people are out there making trouble, too," Dr. Orson said as though I needed reminding. The prytheen *here* might obey Auric, but there were plenty out there who wouldn't. It was a concern that the joint colony would need to do something about soon.

"He'll work on that once he's up and about," I said. "I'll talk to him about it now, if he's up to having a visitor."

It wasn't much of an excuse for seeing him, but it was all I had. Auric's injuries had needed time to heal, and he couldn't afford to vanish into the healing trance like the other prytheen. He'd been leading his people from a hospital bunk, recovering slowly, and Dr. Orson kept me away as much as possible. I was *bad for his recovery*, she'd said.

That she was right didn't make it any easier to stay away.

I tried to catch sight of him in the crowded sick bay, but the door to the isolation room where Orson had stashed Auric was shut. I tried to hide my disappointment.

Dr. Orson grinned, and I caught her gaze slip over my shoulder at something behind me. That was all the warning I had before Auric's strong arms slipped around my waist and he pulled me to him with crushing, wonderful strength. I gasped, the air driven from my lungs and my hands going to his.

"Khara," he whispered in my ear, his voice sending a shiver down my spine. "I have missed holding you."

Several of the injured colonists in the sick bay let out a cheer and I felt my cheeks heat. Pulling away from Auric, I spun to look at him, my heart hammering in my chest. My khara wore an open chested tunic that did nothing to hide his muscular body. The new wounds had closed into scars that made Auric even sexier. And there was a light in his eyes as he looked at me, a shining glorious need that made it hard to breathe.

Every time I saw him it took my breath away. The world seemed to fade out around us and all I could see was him.

Dr. Orson's laugh brought me back and I blushed bright.

"Officially discharged him today," she said, chuckling and stepping back into the sick bay. "He still needs to take it easy, but I can't keep him here forever. I'll leave the pair of you to discuss, ah, colony business. Don't tear his stitches."

I shot her a *look* that did nothing to wipe the amusement off her face and then she vanished, leaving me alone in the corridor with my khara. I bit my lip, feeling a familiar tingle as he took my arm. One problem with running the colony together would be how much we distracted each other. *Going to have to work on that. Eventually.*

Outside the ship, farms were taking shape. Slowly, dangerously slowly given the number of mouths we had to feed, but they were there. Auric looked out at the work being done — mostly by humans, but some prytheen worked amongst them.

"I would not have believed a colony could form so quickly, my love," he said, pulling me into a powerful hug. This time I didn't try to resist — whatever dignity the colony captain should have could go hang. I'd missed him and his touch too much.

"It's pretty much what we'd planned for Arcadia," I said, snuggling into the firm warmth of his chest. "Not really my doing."

"Nonsense," Auric told me firmly. "You are in charge, and this is not the world you set out for. I doubt my Silver Band would have managed anything like this well, and you *will* take the credit you are due."

His tone brooked no argument, and my heart warmed at his words. I'd put a lot of work into this, even if it was hard to accept.

"Your warriors helped," I told him. "They did some of the heavy lifting, and the food they've brought in hunting was a godsend. That left the human colonists free to focus on getting the farms running."

"Together we can make this work." Auric's arm squeezed my shoulders and we looked out at the hills. "I just hope that the other alphas see the benefits of equal cooperation."

"And if they don't?" I asked, shivering slightly. I knew that there might be more hostile prytheen out there, but I didn't want to think about it much.

"If they don't, we'll make them," Auric said. "Do not

worry, my love. I will send emissaries to find them and explain. If I can avoid fighting, I will."

That was as much as I could ask, I realized. And there were more pressing matters on both our minds.

"Dr. Orson gave you a clean bill of health?"

"Of course not," Auric snorted. "She threatened to tie me to a bed if I left now, but she couldn't keep me from your side, my love. I will not be kept from your side just because she doesn't want to let me up."

I punched his arm, with as much effect as punching a tree, and he laughed. "See? If a formidable warrior such as yourself can't hurt me…"

It was hard to contain my laughter at that, but I aimed a more serious punch at him. He swayed back, letting my fist swing through the space he'd vacated, and grabbed me before I caught my balance. I squirmed, helpless and laughing, and he lifted me without paying any attention to my struggles.

"No fair," I gasped.

"I don't intend to be fair," he told me, carrying me into the ship as I struggled playfully. Thankfully there was no chance I'd escape his grip.

Auric didn't put me down on the way to my cabin, carrying me casually, pinning my arms as I squirmed and laughed. "Quiet, or I shall tickle you."

"Oh, and you think that will shut me up?" I protested, only for him to make good on his threat. I shrieked and kicked. "Okay, okay, I give in!"

"Good," he said, pushing open the door to my cabin

and stepping inside. My heart pounded as the door swung shut behind us.

We'd been alone on our journey across the planet, of course. But somehow it was different now that we were on the ship again, surrounded by our people. Now, being with him in this small space seemed almost scandalous. Like the entire crew would know.

Who cares? They know already, I reminded myself as Auric put me down gently. Still, my cheeks heated and I felt almost embarrassed as he looked at me.

That intense gaze made me melt, and I felt the flush spread across my body. Auric breathed in deeply and smiled, a hungry, eager expression.

I forgot about what anyone else might think. Auric was all that mattered, and I stared back at him with the same hunger. Let myself admire him, his taut muscles and broad shoulders, his golden eyes.

Biting my lip, I unzipped my uniform. Auric growled wordlessly, casting off his tunic and watching as I opened my top. My breasts heaved as I breathed deep, and he couldn't tear his eyes off me.

It was still hard to grasp. This man, with all his self-control, was helpless. It took everything he had not to pounce straight away, and I could see his struggle against that urge. It felt so good to know that I had such power over him.

That I, Tamara Joyce, could crack his iron will. I felt a flush spread across my breasts as I bit my lip and stepped closer to him. Met his golden gaze. Reached out to run my fingers over the taut muscles of his chest.

That was too much, even for him. Auric's self-control snapped and he pounced with a roar, pulling my top off. My bra followed, torn open when he couldn't work the fastening quick enough, and then his hands were on me.

Caressing me.

Teasing and squeezing and enjoying me.

I could scarcely breathe, I was so aroused. My body ached for him, needed him in a way that I could hardly understand. I'd been suppressing that need for days, and now I didn't need to. Now, I could have what I wanted.

I could have *him*. Auric, my khara. My mate.

His body felt so good under my fingers, skin smooth over hard muscles, warm and firm and powerful. Powerful hands stroked my skin as I leaned in to kiss his chest, letting myself taste the strange alien flavor of him.

The little groan of pleasure I got from him made my breath catch and a shiver ran through me. Emboldened, I kissed my way down him, over his abs. My fingers found the fastening of his pants, fumbling at it. Figuring it out. Undoing it.

Freeing his cock.

A hungry growl escaped Auric's throat as I stroked his hardening member, enjoying the feel of him. And enjoying his pleasure. There was something powerful about knowing that I could do this to him, and I enjoyed every second of his touch.

Swallowing nervously, I sank down, kissing his cock. It hardened at the touch of my lips and I gasped.

Auric's hands slid through my hair, gently guiding me as I lowered my mouth to him. My lips parted around him and I moaned softly as I took him into my mouth, looking up to meet his eyes.

The joy and love and lust I saw there sent another shiver of need through me as I sucked, feeling him swell in my mouth. The strange alien ridges on his dick felt weird but good as I ran my tongue around them, until Auric's breath grew ragged.

With gentle but irresistible strength, he drew me back from him. Shook his head.

"Not yet," he growled, lifting me and kissing me as he carried me to the bed. His hands pulled at what was left of my uniform, tugging it off me and casting it aside. Where the fastenings resisted him, his claws tore them open, and in seconds I was naked.

He pressed me down into the mattress, his hands running across me, claws scratching over my skin deliciously. I shuddered at his touch, feeling myself melt as he parted my legs, traced across my pinned thighs. Brushed teasingly close to my pussy.

My whole body ached for him, and I reached for his cock again only for him to gently guide my hand away. Now it was his turn, and he refused to be distracted.

Bending over me, his sharp, predator's teeth brushed my skin as he kissed me gently. Softly. His warm touch running over me as he bit my neck, making me writhe as I moaned.

Moving lower, he kissed his way to my breasts, and I arched to offer them to his touch. A dexterous tongue flicked at my nipple as he kissed and sucked and bit, making me whimper with need.

Need that he answered, as his hand slid between my legs again. Fingers parted my slick folds, pressing into me with delicate care. Moaning softly, I arched and spread my legs, my body shaking as his touch drove me wild. Auric knew exactly how to hold me, how to touch me, what would make my body ache and yearn for him.

I'd never been so aroused. His touch was all I felt, fingers and lips and teeth. The sweet almost-pain of his bite as he teased my breasts.

"Auric," I moaned, managing to somehow get words out through the rolling waves of pleasure that threatened to drown my mind. "Auric, please, I need you. I need you inside me."

The low growl that answered me told me Auric wanted it too. Wanted it as badly as I did. He just wasn't going to make it easy for me — he had his plans, and I was helpless in his hands.

His fingers caressed my clit, circling, pressing firmly. Speeding up. My breath came fast and heavy as he pushed me to the brink.

And over.

My shout of joy filled the cabin as I arched under him, shaking and moaning. Clutching at him, pulling him to me.

God, he was good. Better than anything I'd imagined, impossibly good. And he wasn't done with me yet.

I looked up at him, eyes wide, as he positioned himself above me. His wonderful, vibrating alien cock poised at the wet and eager opening of my sex. Auric's face was lit with a bright smile and his hands pressed me down into the mattress, pinning me.

"Now you are ready for me, my love," he said, and his voice echoed in my mind. It was as though I felt his pride, the joy he got from reducing me to a helpless quivering mess of pleasure. And he felt an echo of the ecstasy he woke inside me as he thrust, burying himself deep.

"Oh god!" I cried out, shuddering as he filled me, my pussy squeezing around him. I was already close, so close, and my nails raked his back, urging him on.

He didn't need much encouragement. Our two bodies moved as one, rocking slowly, then faster and faster. The world around us faded away, and when he bit down on my neck again, I screamed his name.

"Auric!" It was a cry of joy, of love, of worship almost. And his answering growl mirrored it, carrying his devotion to me as well as the ecstasy filling him. All control lost, we moved in a frenzy of lust and need and pleasure. I wanted this moment to last forever, to spend the rest of time locked in this embrace with Auric, to never let him go.

"Tamara," he whispered in my ear, voice husky and hungry. "I love you."

I tried to answer, but no words came. Just a gasp of voiceless joy as the two of us shuddered together, and the world dissolved into white light.

The orgasm was incredible, world-shaking. My body shook, new sensations shooting through me, and I could feel him as well. His pleasure, his joy, as the waves of pleasure crashed through him and he came deep inside me.

We rode the orgasm together, wringing every last moment of joy from our joined bodies before collapsing together on the bed. Auric panted beside me, his body slick with sweat and his arms drawing me close. I could scarcely move, but I snuggled into him with a happy little whimper.

It was the closest sound I could make to speech, and I knew he understood. His hand stroked my hair as I rested my head on his chest and we drifted off to sleep together.

I'd never felt happier.

∼

When Mr. Mews eventually woke me, I groaned resentfully and waved at him to shut up. But his insistent noise dragged me up from sleep and I realized I'd slept longer than I'd expected. Much longer.

The virtual cat was doing his job, even if I resented it. I had work to do and so did Auric, if we were ever going to get this colony working. The part of me that remembered my responsibilities wanted to leap up and get back to the work I'd missed.

It was drowned out by the warm feel of Auric beside me, his chest rising and falling under my head. The steady beat of his heart lulled me, pulling me back to sleep. I could rest a little longer, surely.

A loud knock at the door pulled me back to alertness. From the bedside table Mr. Mews gave me a look that said *I tried to warn you*, and I glared back at him.

"What is it?" I called. I couldn't put off my duties forever.

"Captain, you're needed on deck," someone replied. Collins? It might have been Collins, but I couldn't be sure. There were so many new names to remember now. "I mean, if you two are quite finished in there."

His barely suppressed laughter made me flush, but there was nothing mean about it. It warmed my heart a little to hear the playful way he spoke.

I'd worried about how the crew would take my relationship with Auric. It was one thing to ally with the prytheen, but would the other humans accept me sleeping with one? Now I knew that at least some of them would be okay with it. That helped.

Not that I'd let them keep me from him. After what we'd been through, anyone who wanted to keep us apart would have a fight on their hands.

"Whatever he wants can wait," Auric said. I hadn't realized he was awake until he spoke. "They can manage without us for a while longer."

That was very tempting. I looked at my beloved, his

gentle smile and sparkling golden eyes. Yes, we could stay in bed until hunger dragged us out to forage for something to eat. But that wasn't in either of our natures, and we both knew it.

"We're on our way," I called through the door, pulling myself from the bed and Auric's warm embrace with some reluctance. He groaned a complaint but followed, making a face as he got out from under the blanket.

His hands caught me as I pulled on my pants, and I pressed myself back into his embrace for a moment before pulling away again. "We have to go, love. They need us."

"I know," he said. "And there'll be plenty of other chances to catch up. That doesn't mean I won't enjoy watching you now, though."

I giggled. It was impossible to keep my joy hidden as my mate watched me get dressed. The intensity of his gaze left me flushed and flustered and if it hadn't been for the people waiting outside our cabin, I'd have jumped him all over again.

He took my hand, and together we stepped out into the future we would build for our people. Together.

EPILOGUE

Months passed and the deck of the *Wandering Star* was finally full of life, humans and prytheen warriors mixing in the market that had sprung up there. There was still tension, of course — none of the humans had forgotten why we were stranded here, or the deaths that the Silver Band had brought. For their part, the alien hunters were uncomfortable mixing with humans.

But they were *trying*. I smiled down from my spot on the bridge, looking out through the cracked window at farmers and craftsmen trading with prytheen hunters. Explorers returned from the hills, bringing back news of the planet from their travels. There would be trouble between our two species, that was inevitable, but we'd deal with it.

"We still need a name for our new home," Auric said from behind me. It took an effort not to squeal and jump — I doubted I would ever get used to how quietly he moved. I hoped not: it was always a pleasant surprise to be pounced on by him.

Snuggling back into his embrace, I relaxed in the warmth of his loving arms. No matter how long we spent together, I couldn't get enough of his touch.

The issue of a name had come up before: we couldn't keep calling our new home 'the planet' but agreeing on anything else wasn't a high priority. That hadn't stopped people coming up with their own names, though.

"I've heard some of the kids call it Crashland," I said after a while. "Seems appropriate, right?"

Auric laughed, a deep rumble that vibrated through me. "Not the most dignified name, but if people are already calling it that…"

"… better not to try and fight it," I agreed with a smile. "Okay, the Joint Colony of Crashland it is."

"I don't think that's what you called me here to talk about though," my khara said, his lips brushing my neck and making me squirm and moan.

"Are you going to tell me?" he asked, his teeth gently scratching my skin.

"Stop distracting me and I might," I answered with a giggle. Letting out a reluctant sigh, he stopped and let me talk.

"I got news from Dr. Orson this morning," I continued, turning in his arms and looking up at my beloved. "Good news, I hope. She's got to run some more tests to be sure, since she's never seen this before... but I'm pretty sure I'm pregnant."

Auric's brows furrowed at the unfamiliar word and then a light came on in his eyes. His arms tightened around me and he lifted me high with a joyous whoop.

"I'm going to be a father?" Spinning around, he laughed and put me down with exaggerated care. "I'm going to be a father!"

Wonder mixed with his joy and he leaned in to kiss me gently but thoroughly.

"I wasn't sure that would be possible," he said when our lips parted. "I hardly dared hope."

I rested my head against his broad blue chest, relieved. "I'm glad that you're happy, Auric. I worried—"

"—that I might be an idiot?" He chuckled, squeezing me gently. "Of course I'm delighted, my khara. I want nothing more than to be a good father to our kits."

I smiled, and then frowned. "Wait, kits, *plural?* How many are you expecting?"

"Three or four, most likely," he said, sounding a little puzzled. "Why do you ask?"

Oh boy.

The End

Thank you for reading *Auric!* Please take a moment to leave an opinion about the book, I appreciate every review.

Torran**, book 2 of the *****Crashland Colony Romances*****, is out now! Click here to get it.**

**If you'd like to hear more about my upcoming releases, and get a free novella, sign up for my mailing list:
http://my.leslie-chase.com/booksignup**

CRASHLAND SAGA

CRASHLAND COLONY ROMANCES

Auric

Crashed on an unexplored planet, with only an alien warrior and a holographic cat for company... what's a girl to do?

Torran

Stranded on the wrong planet, captured by brutal alien raiders, the only good thing about Lisa's situation is Torran. He's a dangerous alien warrior - who also happens to be the hottest man she's ever met. Strong, protective, and lethal, he's everything she could want or need.

Perhaps she shouldn't have shot him on sight?

Ronan

Trapped with a sexy alien warrior, a holographic owl, and a mystery she needs to solve. Becca doesn't like the prytheen, she doesn't trust them, and she is absolutely not interested in this one.

So why is she having so much trouble keeping her hands off him?

CRASHLAND CASTAWAY ROMANCES

BOUND TO THE ALIEN BARBARIAN

Crashed on the wrong planet.

Stuck with the wrong man.

Taken by the right alien.

Waking up to find she's one of only two humans to survive a crash is bad. Being captured by an alien warrior who isn't sure if she's a demon is worse. But when the alien claims her as his mate, she doesn't know if she wants to escape…

∼

CHAINED TO THE ALIEN CHAMPION

Marakz is the hottest man I've ever seen. Also the most infuriating. At least Lord Pouncington likes him…

Diplomatic contact between the Joint Colony and the Zrin gets off to a rocky start when the Sri champion sees his mate amongst the humans. When disaster strikes, she's his first thought — but is he rescuing her or capturing her?

Megan isn't sure she cares.

∼

TIED TO THE ALIEN TYRANT

Trapped on the Wrong World. Captured by an Alien Warlord. A *Super-Sexy* Alien Warlord…

The alien warlord is trouble. Dangerous, ambitious, deadly trouble. Worst of all, he's *smart*. Between that and his rugged jaw, rippling muscles, and intense eyes, he makes me melt every time he looks my way. I should be planning my escape, finding a way back to the colony. Instead, all I can think about is what his blue skin will feel like.

Tzaron may be the toughest, most handsome man within a thousand lightyears, but he's still the barbarian warlord who captured me.

He says he needs me for my technical skills, but I know better. Every smoldering glance, every touch of his skin, even the tone of his voice tells me he wants more. He wants *me*.

And the worst thing is, the longer I'm his prisoner, the less I want to escape.

ABOUT LESLIE CHASE

LESLIE CHASE

I love writing, and especially enjoy writing sexy science fiction and paranormal romances. It lets my imagination run free and my ideas come to life! When I'm not writing, I'm busy thinking about what to write next or researching it – yes, damn it, looking at castles and swords and spaceships counts as research.

If you enjoy my books, please let me know with a review. Reviews are really important and I appreciate every one. If you'd like to be kept up to date on my new releases, you can sign up for my email newsletter through my website. Every subscriber gets a free science fiction romance ebook!

www.leslie-chase.com

facebook.com/lesliechaseauthor
twitter.com/lchasewrites
bookbub.com/authors/leslie-chase

SCI FI ROMANCE BY LESLIE CHASE

DRAGONS OF MARS

The remains of the Dragon Empire have slumbered on Mars for a thousand years, but now the ancient shifters are awake, alive, and searching for their mates!

Each book can be read on its own, but you'll get the best effect if you read them in order.

- **Dragon Prince's Mate**
- **Dragon Pirate's Prize**
- **Dragon Guardian's Match**
- **Dragon Lord's Hope**
- **Dragon Warrior's Heart**

WORLDWALKER BARBARIANS

Teleported from Earth to a far-off planet, found by blue skinned wolf-shifter aliens, and claimed as mates. Is this disaster or delight for the feisty human females?

1: Zovak

2: Davor

SILENT EMPIRE BOOKS

Romance in a Galactic Empire

Each of these books follows the story of a different woman, snatched from Earth and thrust into the Silent Empire — a galaxy-spanning nation of intrigue and romance. Read to see them find their alien mates amongst the stars.

Each of these books can be read as a standalone, though they share some characters.

- **STOLEN FOR THE ALIEN PRINCE**
- **STOLEN BY THE ALIEN RAIDER**
- **STOLEN BY THE ALIEN GLADIATOR**

THE ALIEN EXPLORER'S LOVE

Can Two Beings from Different Worlds Find Common Ground — And Love?

Jaranak is an alien explorer on a rescue mission to Earth, but now he's stranded here at the dawn of the 20th century. And his efforts to go unnoticed are bring thwarted by Lilly, a human female who won't stop asking questions. She should be insufferable, but instead he finds himself unable to get the sassy woman out of his mind…

MATED TO THE ALIEN LORD

a Celestial Mates novel by Leslie Chase

Love is never easy. Love on an alien world is downright dangerous!

With her life on Earth going nowhere, Gemma needs a fresh start. Enter the Celestial Mates Agency, who say they can match her with the perfect alien. And despite the dangers of his planet, Corvax is everything she could have asked for — impossibly hot, brave, and huge.

Now that she's seen him, there's no way she's going back.

PARANORMAL ROMANCE BY LESLIE CHASE

ARCANE AFFAIRS AGENCY

A shared world of shifters, vampires, far, and witches - full of everything that goes bump in the night! Check out the full list of books **here**.

THE BEAR AND THE HEIR, by Leslie Chase

When Cole North arrives in Argent Falls to investigate reports of magical storms, he doesn't expect much to come of it. Not after the series of pointless missions the Arcane Affairs Agency has sent him on recently. This time, though, it's different. The small town is plagued by bizarre weather, the storms are trying to warn him off, and there are *fae* running wild. And then there's Fiona.

No matter how much the bear shifter tries to focus on his mission, he can't get the hot, curvy girl out of his head. But the fae are after her too – and when they try and kidnap her, Cole's mission and his feelings for Fiona collide.

GUARDIAN BEARS

Ex-military bear shifters providing protection from the threats no one else can deal with. Each book is a stand-alone plot, as the sexy bears find their curvy mates.

1. Guardian Bears: Marcus
2. Guardian Bears: Lucas
3. Guardian Bears: Karl

~

TIGER'S SWORD

A four-part paranormal romance serial about Maxwell Walters, billionaire tiger shifter, and his curvy mate Lenore.

Box Set, collecting all four parts

1. **Tiger's Hunt**
2. **Tiger's Den**
3. **Tiger's Claws**
4. **Tiger's Heart**

Printed in Great Britain
by Amazon